The
Chocolate
Cupid
Killings

The
Chocolate
Cupid
Killings

·A Chocoholic Mystery·

JoAnna Carl

AN OBSIDIAN MYSTERY

OBSIDIAN
Published by New American Library, a division of
Penguin Group (USA) Inc., 375 Hudson Street,
New York, New York 10014, USA
Penguin Group (Canada), 90 Eglinton Avenue East, Suite 700, Toronto,
Ontario M4P 2Y3, Canada (a division of Pearson Penguin Canada Inc.)
Penguin Books Ltd., 80 Strand, London WC2R 0RL, England
Penguin Ireland, 25 St. Stephen's Green, Dublin 2,
Ireland (a division of Penguin Books Ltd.)
Penguin Group (Australia), 250 Camberwell Road, Camberwell, Victoria 3124,
Australia (a division of Pearson Australia Group Pty. Ltd.)
Penguin Books India Pvt. Ltd., 11 Community Centre, Panchsheel Park,
New Delhi - 110 017, India
Penguin Group (NZ), 67 Apollo Drive, Rosedale, North Shore 0632,
New Zealand (a division of Pearson New Zealand Ltd.)
Penguin Books (South Africa) (Pty.) Ltd., 24 Sturdee Avenue,
Rosebank, Johannesburg 2196, South Africa

Penguin Books Ltd., Registered Offices:
80 Strand, London WC2R 0RL, England

First published by Obsidian, an imprint of New American Library,
a division of Penguin Group (USA) Inc.

First Printing, October 2009
10 9 8 7 6 5 4 3 2 1

LIBRARY OF CONGRESS CATALOGING-IN-PUBLICATION DATA:

Carl, JoAnna.
The chocolate cupid killings: a chocoholic mystery/JoAnna Carl.
p. cm.
ISBN 978-0-451-22797-3
1. McKinney, Lee (Fictitious character)—Fiction. 2. Confectioners—Fiction. 3. Women
detectives—Michigan—Fiction. 4. City and town life—Michigan—Fiction. I. Title.
PS3569.A51977C483 2010
813'54—dc22   2009017655

Set in Stempel Garamond
Designed by Alissa Amell

Printed in the United States of America

For my special pals,
Sherry, Louisa, and Linda

Acknowledgments

As ever, thanks are due to many people who helped with this book. Foremost are my Michigan neighbors: Susan McDermott, Tracy Paquin, and Dick Trull. Lawmen Jim Avance and Robert "Officer Bob" Swartz were kind and informative. My daughters and sons-in-law, Betsy and Sam Peters and Ruth and Bart Henson, and my son, John Sandstrom, answered many questions at moments that were convenient for me, but not always for them. Holland, Michigan, librarian Robin Williams-Voight, was a great help. And Dr. Marty Ludlum purchased the right to have his name—not his appearance or personality!—used in this book with a generous contribution to the Lawton, Oklahoma, Arts for All drive.

I'd also like to thank my agent, Maureen Walters, and my editor, Tracy Bernstein, for their unfailing help and encouragement.

The
Chocolate
Cupid
Killings

Chapter 1

The name on the stranger's ID card may have read Valentine, but he was no cupid.

Cupid is little, round, and cute, and this guy was tall, skinny, and ugly. He definitely didn't look as if he could flit around on a tiny pair of wings; he clunked into TenHuis Chocolade in heavy snow boots that seemed to be bigger than they needed to be. And he wasn't wearing Cupid's airy draperies. His scrawny neck stuck out of a parka shaped like a turtle's shell covered with cheap nylon and trimmed with fur from some polyester beast.

I had Valentines, cupids, hearts, and arrows on the brain because it was the first week in February, and our retail shop was decked with items celebrating Valentine's Day. Our workshop, of course, was way out ahead of that season. The highly skilled people back there—the ones I call the "hairnet ladies"—were producing Easter bunnies and eggs, tiny chocolate chicks, and Mother's Day roses.

We don't have much walk-in business in the winter; summer is the busy season for Lake Michigan beach resorts like Warner Pier. As business manager, I was handling the counter myself, so I left my office to wait on the customer. He didn't look like the romantic type, but if he had a sweetheart I was willing to sell him a pound of our handmade European-style bonbons and truffles.

Before I could offer to help him, he flipped that identification card out on the counter. "Derrick Valentine," he said. His voice croaked, and he smelled like cigarettes. When he opened his mouth, I expected smoke to pour out. "I'm with PDQ Investigations. Do you have a Christina Meachum working here?"

His hand hovered over the ID card, partly hiding it, but I picked it up and read it carefully. The only additional information I learned was that PDQ Investigations had an Atlanta address. The card didn't seem to be issued by any official agency.

"As I'm sure you're aware," I said, "we're limited in what information we can hand out about our employees. But that's no problem this time, because there is no Christina Meachum listed on our payola. I mean, payroll!"

Rats! I'd twisted my tongue. At least Derrick Valentine didn't know me. He wouldn't realize I usually did that when I was nervous.

"Maybe you've seen her." Valentine dropped a photograph onto the counter.

The picture was of terrible quality. It had been blown up from a driver's license or some other ID card. It showed a woman with dark hair worn in a medium-length bob, parted on the side. Her eyes were dark and expertly made up, but her stare was blank. Her face was heart-shaped, her mouth small and pouting. Only her eyes were noticeable, and that was because of the makeup.

I frowned at the picture. "I'm sorry," I said. "She's a com-

mon type, of course, but I can't help you. Why are you looking for her?"

"It's a legal matter."

"She's wanted by the police?"

"Civil case." Valentine reached inside his cheap parka. "I'll
leave a business card. I'd appreciate a call if she shows up."

"Why do you think she might be here? Is she a big fan of
expensive chocolate?"

"She has experience in food service. And we have information that she's been in this area of Michigan." Valentine gestured at our decorated counters. "While I'm here, maybe I
ought to get some candy for my wife."

I didn't correct his terminology—we make "chocolate,"
not "candy." I just handed him a list of our flavors with the
price per pound marked prominently at the top. Our chocolates are expensive; I never want to fill a box without making
sure the customer knows ahead of time just how much it's
going to cost.

"While you're looking this over, I need to give the workroom a message," I said. "I'll be right back."

I went to the door to the workshop and called out, "Aunt
Nettie!"

My aunt, who owns TenHuis Chocolade and who is in
charge of making our luscious chocolates, turned. "Yes, Lee."

"There's a problem with the sugar organ. I mean, order!
We need to talk about the sugar order as soon as you're free."

"I'll be there in a minute." Aunt Nettie—a chunky descen-
dant of west Michigan's Dutch pioneers—turned to one of her
crew, Pamela Thompson. "Please go to the back storeroom
and get a tray of eight-ounce bunnies. The ones carrying
baskets."

Pamela was one of our newer employees. Her blond hair was covered with a heavy white food service hairnet, and she wore a white smock like all the other women who make our fabulous bonbons and truffles. She stopped wrapping Easter eggs in cellophane and obeyed Aunt Nettie without a word.

I went back to the counter, and at Derrick Valentine's instruction filled a half-pound box with Italian Cherry bonbons ("Amareena cherries in white chocolate cream filling encased in a dark chocolate heart") and Amaretto truffles ("A milk chocolate interior flavored with almond liqueur and coated with white chocolate"). I tied the box with red ribbon, then embellished it with a dangling cupid—plastic covered with gold paint. The private eye paid his bill and left, and I went back into my office, which has glass walls so that I can see what's going on in the workroom and in the shop.

I could also see parts of the quaint shopping district outside our big front window. I watched as Derrick Valentine of PDQ Investigations crossed the street, walked to the corner, leaned against the show window of Peach Street Antiques, and lit a cigarette.

Was he watching TenHuis Chocolade? I tried not to stare at him. I didn't know whether or not he could see me through our big front window.

Aunt Nettie slid into my office, looking nervous. "Who was that man?"

"He's a private eye. He was looking for a Christina Meachum."

She relaxed visibly and adjusted the white net over her blond-white hair. "That's okay, then."

"No, it's not okay. Christina Meachum was the name, but the photo he showed me was a 'before' picture of Pamela."

We looked at each other seriously. Neither of us knew just what to do.

Pamela was a special employee.

Only a couple of months earlier had I been allowed to learn something that Aunt Nettie had known for much longer. One of her closest friends, Sarajane Harding, was involved in that mysterious underground railway system that helps abused women permanently escape from their abusers by furnishing them with new identities and finding them new homes.

Sarajane, Aunt Nettie told me, had herself formerly been an abused wife. Because she ran one of Warner Pier's best bed-and-breakfast inns, she could provide temporary lodging without causing comment about strange people coming and going, and she was often called on to house these unfortunate women briefly.

This "underground railway" system is not like the shelters for abused women found in most cities. It is not used for women who simply need to escape a violent husband or lover until things cool down or until they can take legal action. Sarajane was involved in much more serious cases, cases in which the railway "conductors" believed the women were in danger of death, in which the only option seen for them was a new identity, a new life in a new place. If strange men came looking for them, there was a strong possibility that those men were dangerous.

Normally Aunt Nettie would not take part in this activity. For one thing, its legality may be questioned, since it won't work without creating fake IDs, and Aunt Nettie is married to Warner Pier's chief of police. Hogan Jones, her husband of less than a year, might close his eyes to the situation briefly—he despises abusive husbands—but he couldn't ignore it permanently. So Aunt Nettie and Sarajane were careful not to let him know what was going on.

I'd also been careful not to mention Pamela and her problems to my husband, Joe Woodyard. After all, he is Warner Pier's city attorney, on the days when he's not restoring antique powerboats. I didn't want to put him in a bad position either. What he didn't know wouldn't hurt him.

Pamela was the second of Sarajane's passengers who had needed a job from TenHuis Chocolade. I'm sure Sarajane had employed some women at the B&B, but she had never asked us to hire one until right before Christmas, and that woman worked only a week. Since the women had to be paid off the books, the accountant in me didn't like it, but it's hard to turn your back on people in this much trouble.

Sarajane hadn't told me Pamela's story, but she had made it clear that her danger was real. That was why Aunt Nettie and I had come up with the "sugar order" alert. If I called out to Aunt Nettie that I needed to talk to her about the "sugar order," Pamela was immediately to hide in the back room or the storage closet.

"At least our system worked," Aunt Nettie said. "Pamela's still in the back. Should I call her out?"

"No! That private eye is standing across the street."

Aunt Nettie didn't turn to look at him. "Do you think he's watching the shop?"

"I don't know. He may have only stopped for a smoke. But we'd better take precautions."

"I'll call Sarajane to come and get Pamela."

"That might not be a good idea. After all, Sarajane's car says PEACH STREET BED-AND-BREAKFAST on the side. Besides, I wouldn't want this guy to get a look at Pamela's face as she left. She doesn't look much like her original picture anymore, but I wouldn't want him to see what she does look like."

"Then I can take Pamela out to the B&B. I'm parked in the alley."

"Maybe we should check and make sure there's no one watching the alley."

Aunt Nettie looked dismayed. "I just wanted to help Pamela out with a job for a little while. I didn't mean to get mixed up in some cloak-and-dagger project."

"I'm probably being overly cautious, but let's keep Pamela out of sight for an hour or so. Don't let her come back into the workroom."

"I can have her tie bows."

I nodded. Pamela was one of twenty-five women working at TenHuis Chocolade. None of the others knew who she was or why she had suddenly joined the staff, and we couldn't let them find out. Twenty-five people cannot keep a secret. So that afternoon Pamela had to have a job that kept her out of sight of the street and of our retail shop, but kept her busy doing something that wouldn't make the other employees wonder what was up. Tying bows was a sufficiently dull job that no one would think Pamela was getting special treatment.

I sighed. "Okay. Pamela ties bows. You watch the front, and I'll run to the Superette for Amaretto."

"How did you know we need Amaretto?"

"I didn't. I just suggested it because it's something we buy locally."

"I tried to make a new batch of Amaretto truffles this morning, and there wasn't enough in the bottle to do it."

"Good. I'll go get some, and as I go I can scout the downtown to make sure nobody's watching the alley. Then you can call Sarajane and ask her to get Pamela out of here. She'll probably want to move her along someplace else."

I cast a longing glance at my computer—I didn't really have time to leave my regular work for a scouting trip—put on my ski jacket and left by the front door. In the winter there's plenty of parking on Warner Pier streets, and I hadn't bothered to drive around to the alley where Aunt Nettie and I have reserved spaces. At the corner I turned onto Peach Street, paying no attention to Derrick Valentine. I drove along slowly, looking around as I passed the entrance to our alley. I didn't see anybody suspicious. At first. I was halfway down the block before I saw the man in the plain vanilla sedan.

The sedan was parked across from the end of the alley. The man was sitting there, talking on a cell phone. He had what looked like a map spread out on his steering wheel. He would have a clear view down our alley in his rearview mirror. Was he some innocent salesman, talking to his boss about calling on a Warner Pier business? Or was he tag-teaming Derrick Valentine, making sure no one who looked like Pamela came out our back door?

One thing about a town of twenty-five hundred: a stranger stands out. In the summer, you could hide a battalion of private eyes in the crowds of tourists who throng the quaint streets of Warner Pier. But in wintertime we locals know everyone we see. And I'd never seen this guy around. Plus, his car had a Georgia license plate. As in Atlanta, headquarters of PDQ Investigations.

Aha!

When I returned from the Superette, I parked in front of TenHuis Chocolade once more, got out clutching my bottle of Amaretto and walked though the shop and the workroom and into the back room. I tried to look as un-secretive as I could.

Aunt Nettie has made the break room as pleasant as possible for our employees. It looks like a dining room in a home. The tables and chairs might be from a secondhand store, but they were good-quality traditional pieces to begin with. The chairs have upholstered seats, and prints or paintings by local artists are hung here and there. The kitchen nook has more than a microwave and a refrigerator; a real range with oven and burners is available. There is—oh, glory!—a dishwasher. And that dishwasher isn't for chocolate-making equipment. Those utensils are cleaned in a separate area in the workshop itself.

Pamela was sitting at the largest table. She was surrounded by rolls of ribbon in Easter pastels and a bowl of the little gold bunnies. A can of Pepsi stood off to one side, safe from expansive gestures. Beside it was a small tube of M&M Minis. I bit my tongue at the sight. Pamela consistently refused to eat TenHuis chocolates—some of the best truffles and bonbons in the world—but seemed to be addicted to those M&M Minis, mass-market candies available at every drugstore, supermarket, and convenience store. She always had one or two tubes in her purse or pocket. I knew I was being petty, but it irked me.

Pamela seemed to be irked at me in turn. "I hope this hasn't been a false alarm," she said. "I hate making bows."

I mentally compared Pamela to the picture Derrick Valentine had identified as "Christina Meachum." In the photo, Christina had looked younger. She had been plain, true, but she'd looked normal. Her face was symmetrical.

Pamela's face had a different look, not abnormal exactly, but not like the photo. Her face was skewed, crooked. She talked out of one side of her mouth, and one of her eyebrows was higher than the other.

Christina had dark hair. Pamela's was a brassy, home-dyed blond, part of her attempt to change her appearance. She had lost an eyetooth since the earlier photo had been taken. But she and the woman in the photo had the same narrow chin, if you ignored the lump on the right side of the jaw, and the bright lipstick Pamela wore was smeared over a pouty mouth just like Christina's. The dark eyes were the same shape, and Pamela wore eye makeup like Christina's.

Yes, I felt sure the picture showed Pamela as she had looked before an angry husband had beaten her face out of shape and broken her jaw.

"The detective was looking for someone named Christina Meachum and showed me an old photo," I said. "But—I didn't question that it was you when I saw it. Besides, it would be a pretty big coincidence if some detective was looking for a woman who looked that much like you right in the same area where you were hiding out."

Pamela smirked.

That was the last reaction I had expected. I'm sure I looked astonished, because Pamela immediately dropped her head into her hands.

"I forget what I look like these days," she said. "You're being tactful, trying not to say the picture looked the way I was before I was beaten to a pulp."

Pamela kept her face down, and she used her hands to push her hair back, displaying a broad forehead. She nervously pulled off her hairnet, then put it on again. She pulled it down to help her hair hide her large ears. It was just as well that her disguise required that she cover them up.

I got a Diet Coke out of the refrigerator and sat down opposite her.

"We're eager to see you get started again in life, Pamela. This guy may have had nothing to do with you. But there's a strange car at the end of the alley, too. It would be foolhardy—"

"I know! I know!"

She looked up, letting her hair fall back into a curtain that covered her jaws and forehead. Her eyes looked fierce. "I realize you've jimmied your accounting around for me. I do appreciate it. I just don't see how they could have found me here in Warner Pier."

"The detective said they had information that you'd been in this area. Had you ever been here before?"

Pamela shook her head.

I went on. "Do you have relatives around here? Had you vacationed here? Did you know anybody around here?"

She kept shaking her head. When I'd used up my supply of questions, I stood up. "Aunt Nettie can call Sarajane, and we'll figure a safe way to get you out of here. I'll pay you through today out of petty cash, in case she's able to move you to a safer location."

Pamela's eyes popped open. "A safer location! You mean in another place?"

"That would make sense to me."

"No!" The word shrilled out. "No! I'm not leaving Warner Pier."

Chapter 2

I'm sure I looked amazed. I certainly felt amazed.

Sarajane had gone through the whole rigmarole of sneaking Pamela into Warner Pier, keeping her under cover, helping to change her appearance with a bad bleach job, finding her an off-the-books job, and keeping her true identity secret—even from Aunt Nettie and me—and Pamela was willing to risk staying here when her whereabouts might have been discovered? She could be throwing all Sarajane's work away. And her own life.

Even Aunt Nettie and I had gone to a certain amount of trouble to keep Pamela safe and her identity a secret. And now, when her hideout might be compromised and the violent husband she had fled might be close to finding her, she didn't want to leave Warner Pier.

Yes, I was amazed. Warner Pier was a nice town, but not worth dying over.

Finally Pamela spoke. "I'm just so tired of running." She dropped her head to her hands again.

Maybe I could understand that. "Aunt Nettie is going to call Sarajane," I said. "We'll see what she says." I left without making any other comment.

Pamela pouted, but she kept on tying bows until five o'clock, our closing time in the winter.

As the women of the work crew went out, I took a look through the front window. Derrick Valentine was still across the street, although he'd gotten cold enough to move into the antique shop. The lights were on inside, and I could see him peeking through the back of a Windsor chair. When I found an excuse to take a look down the alley, the car with the Georgia license plate was still across the street.

By that time Sarajane had arranged for a quiet exit for Pamela. She had contacted George Jenkins, owner of a Warner Pier art gallery. George is also involved in the underground railroad, though he and Sarajane don't usually work together.

After everyone had left but Pamela, Aunt Nettie, and me, I called George. He wrapped up a large painting from his gallery, put on his hooded jacket, got into the van with PEACH STREET ART GALLERY on the side, and drove the two blocks to TenHuis Chocolade. He carried the painting in through the front door with no attempt at secrecy and took it back to our break room, which is not visible from the street. He took off his jacket and hung the painting on our north wall. Then he wrapped up the smaller painting it replaced. Both he and Pamela were wearing dark slacks. Pamela put on his jacket, pulled the hood up, walked out the front door holding the second painting in front of her face, loaded it in the van, and drove to the gallery.

Sarajane met her there. We figured Pamela's pursuer must not know where she was living, or he would have gone directly to the B&B.

As soon as the pantomime had gotten Pamela on her way,

George Jenkins put on a different jacket and hat, one he had used as padding for the painting he was lending us. Aunt Nettie stuffed Pamela's own jacket and hat into a large plastic bag. George and Aunt Nettie went out the back door. She was to drive him down various Warner Pier streets and alleys, making sure no one was following them, then deliver him and Pamela's jacket to the back door of his shop.

I left the question of Pamela staying in Warner Pier up to Sarajane. I was only a bystander, after all. But I breathed a sigh of relief as she left. Pamela was away from TenHuis Chocolade, and I hoped she wasn't coming back.

I wasn't due to meet Joe for dinner until six thirty, so I went into my office and worked on my e-mail. At six fifteen I turned on the lights we leave burning at night and got my coat. This was the one afternoon a week Joe actually occupies his city attorney's desk—he does other work evenings and during other odd moments—and I was supposed to meet him at City Hall. We had a big evening planned. We were going to his mother's house for dinner, and the evening had the earmarks of being an important occasion.

Joe's mom, Mercy Woodyard, had invited Joe and me and our good friends Lindy and Tony Herrera, but not their kids. Mercy's boyfriend, Mike Herrera, mayor of Warner Pier—who happens to be Tony's dad—was also to be there.

As I said, Warner Pier is a small town, so we had overlapping relationships with all these people. As mayor, Mike Herrera was Joe's boss. He dated Joe's mom. Lindy Herrera and I had been close friends since we were sixteen, the year we both worked as summer counter girls for TenHuis Chocolade. Lindy had married Mike Herrera's son. Tony Herrera had been a friend of Joe's since high school. Joe's mom was the proprietor of our town's only insurance agency, and Mike Herrera owned three restaurants in Warner Pier, so both were members of our small business community. Lindy was catering manager for her father-in-law. If you drew a diagram of how we were all related by friendship, blood, work, and marriage, it would look like something a four-year-old scribbled with crayons.

We all saw a lot of one another, but neither Lindy, Tony, Joe, nor I could remember being invited to an adults-only dinner at Joe's mom's house. After all, Mike Herrera owned three restaurants. If we all got together it was usually in one of them. And if this was an informal family gathering, why weren't Tony and Lindy's three children included?

Something was definitely up.

Mike and Mercy had each been widowed for a long time, and they'd been seeing each other at least three years. They maintained separate domiciles, but they'd taken the occasional trip together and they frequently were in each other's homes quite late. Like all night. As their adult children, we were careful not to ask too many questions.

Anyway, tonight's dinner had all the atmosphere of a formal announcement.

We were all happy about it, at least outwardly. In fact, I think Tony, Lindy, and I were all thrilled and pleased. But Joe's reaction to the invitation had been—well, not exactly unenthusiastic. Cautious might be a better term.

"It's going to mean big changes for me," he said.

"Why?"

"I'll have to quit my city job," he said. "Nepotism. Mike can't hire his stepson."

"Mike didn't hire you. The city council did."

"Yeah, but Mike proposed my employment. There's already been a lot of talk about it around town."

"But you've worked like a dog for the city! You can't quit because of gossip."

"It's not because of gossip, Lee. I think Mike is a good mayor. I'd like to see him serve at least one more term, to get his economic development program under way before he leaves office. I'm afraid that he's going to say he won't run again, rather than let me resign."

I thought that over. "Well, it's only a part-time job, Joe. The boat shop is doing better financially, and my salary at TenHuis Chocolade has improved. We can get along without that job."

Joe laughed. "I'm not unemployable. Several law firms— and even the FBI—tried to recruit me out of law school, you know!"

"I can't see you as an FBI agent. You're too antiestablishment."

"A city attorney is part of the establishment. I guess I've been converted. Anyway, I can find another job of some kind."

"Part-time?"

"Maybe it's time to think about something full-time."

If Joe took a full-time job, he'd have to sell the boat shop, and he loved the boat shop.

I had asked more questions, but Joe didn't want to answer them. He had said his ideas were too vague to talk about. I had dropped the matter. For then.

Now I remembered the discussion as I locked the shop's door behind myself. Joe is a man of many virtues, but he has one fault. He keeps things to himself. This can be quite annoying to a wife, but I had resolved not to nag. I'd learned that when Joe has a problem, he wants to turn it over in his mind. After he works it out, he explains. I was hoping he'd explain soon.

TenHuis Chocolade is three blocks from the Warner Pier City Hall. The sun had gone down long before, of course, but Warner Pier is perfectly safe any time of the day or night. I decided to walk over to meet Joe.

I had moved from Dallas to my mother's hometown only three years earlier, and so far I found the Michigan winters stimulating. It was nice to walk past the Victorian buildings of Warner Pier. The temperature was dropping toward the teens, but I had a ski jacket, a knitted hat, wool pants, boots, and gloves. And, unlike Texas, Michigan has little wind. I took deep breaths of the cold air and felt myself relax.

Warner Pier City Hall occupies a charming Victorian house with a wide porch. I didn't climb onto the porch; I knew the main public entrance would be closed, though there were a couple of cars—a nondescript sedan and a flashy SUV—in the slots set aside for visitor parking.

I followed a sidewalk around to the side, to a door marked POLICE DEPARTMENT. That door is also locked after five o'clock, when 9-1-1 service is taken over by the sheriff's dispatcher, thirty miles away in the county seat, and the lone patrolman on duty is out in his car. But the door was close to Joe's desk; he would hear me knock.

The Warner Pier PD isn't protected with bulletproof glass or a fancy electronic security system. After all, there are only four members of the department, five if you count the secretary who doubles as the daytime dispatcher. Hogan Jones, Aunt Nettie's husband, is chief over three patrolmen. This might seem to be a comedown for a man who retired as one of the top detectives in the Cincinnati, Ohio, Police Department. But Hogan seems to enjoy the slow pace of Warner Pier law enforcement.

The door to the WPPD has a heavy glass panel in its upper half, and inside the panel is a Venetian blind. After hours that blind is closed. But that evening the blind was still open. In fact, there were lots of lights inside. Was something going on?

I pulled on the door, and it swung open. No one had locked up. That was odd, but it didn't necessarily mean anything, I told myself. Hogan could have simply lost track of the time.

I walked into the small entrance area. I could see the entire police station from there. Hogan's office door was closed, and the rest of the place was deserted. Even the door to the one little holding cell stood open, and I could see the empty bunk inside.

I shrugged. Then I walked through the swinging gate that signaled that callers should halt by the reception desk, and I turned down the short hall leading to the little room where Joe has a desk.

The room was too small to be an office. It was more like a storage closet. It was strictly utilitarian—metal desk, tile floor, computer screen. Joe's desk was littered with papers, which meant he wasn't through working. He always filed things away and made neat stacks before he left.

There was no one in the tiny space, no Joe at the desk.

I tried the door that led to the city clerk's office and the other offices toward the front of the building. It was locked.

I went back into the police department. Where was Joe? If

he had to leave, why hadn't he called me? If the police station had shut down for the day, why wasn't the door locked? Should I call Joe's cell phone?

The only closed door was the one to Hogan's office. Could Joe and Hogan be in there? But why? They were friends as well as shirttail relations, and they frequently talked, but I'd never known them to do it behind closed doors. And I wouldn't have expected them to leave the outer door of the police station open when the main office was empty.

I walked over to the door and listened. I heard the rumble of a voice, then an answer from a different voice. I couldn't make out the words, but there were definitely two guys in there.

I felt relieved. They must be having some sort of bull session.

I gave a perfunctory knock. Then I turned the handle and threw the door open. "So y'all are hiding in here! Don't you know it's time to go home?"

I was facing a completely strange man. He was tall and completely bald, with a face that looked as if he had lost a dozen bar fights. I'd never seen him before in my life.

Then I realized that Joe and Hogan were in the office, too. And so were two other strangers—city guys wearing dressy dark overcoats. They were big guys.

Five big men were packed into Hogan's minuscule office as tightly as I'd pack thirty-two Dutch caramel bonbons into a one-pound gift box.

I was gaping, and all five of the men were gaping wider than I was.

Three of us spoke at once. "I'm sorry!" I said.

"Oh, hell!" Joe said.

"Hi, Lee." That was Hogan.

The strange men kept quiet, but Joe, Hogan, and I again began to talk at the same time.

I said, "I didn't know I was interpreting. I mean, interrupting!"

Joe said, "I forgot we were going to dinner at Mom's!"

Hogan said, "We're still tied up."

The big ugly man turned his back on the rest of us and studied a hall tree in the corner of Hogan's office. If he was trying to be inconspicuous, it didn't work. There was nothing on that hall tree but a heavy and extremely unattractive navy blue jacket with WPPD in bright yellow letters on the front and back.

The two men in city clothes also ducked their heads as if they were trying to look inconspicuous. All I could see of them were neatly trimmed heads—one dark, one fair—and a set of extremely bushy eyebrows on the darker man.

I barely gave them a glance. The big ugly man's behavior was so odd that I couldn't help staring at him. "I'll wait at your desk, Joe," I said.

I turned and stepped out of Hogan's office, closing the door. But it reopened immediately. Joe followed me out and closed the door behind him. Firmly. He took my arm.

"I'm sorry I interrupted," I said. "I heard y'all talking . . ."

Joe was frowning. "Not your fault. I should have remembered you were coming and called to head you off."

"Head me off?"

"Right. I can't leave. You'll have to give my excuses."

"Give your excuses? But, Joe, this is *your* mom who called a big meeting of the clans. I'm just an in-law!"

"Sorry. But Hogan wants me to stay."

I was dumbfounded. Joe's work as city attorney has nothing to do with crime. His main function is to look over city policies and ordinances to make sure they're legal. Hogan enforces the law, not Joe.

"Joe, what is going on?"

"Nothing, Lee. Hogan just wants me to sit in on a meeting."

"I'll tell your mom you'll be late."

"No! I don't think I'll be through here for— Well, it could be midnight."

"Midnight!" If I sounded exasperated, it was only because I *was* exasperated. "You can't bow out on this family meeting. It's too important to your mom."

Joe's face looked like thunder. "It's not because I'm not interested, Lee. You'll just have to represent us."

Before I could marshal a new argument, he was moving me toward the outside door.

"Joe!" I protested, but he kept moving me along. "Joe, your mom is not going to like this!"

We were at the door, and Joe swung it open. "Sorry, Lee. I can't come."

I was outside. The door closed behind me.

Then it abruptly opened again. About three inches. Joe spoke through the crack. "Don't tell anyone about this." His voice made it an order.

Then the door slammed shut. I heard the lock click. I pressed my nose against the glass.

Joe closed the Venetian blind in my face.

If I'd been amazed when I walked in on the private meeting, that was nothing to the way I felt now. My husband had thrown me out. Into the dark.

I considered picking up a rock and tossing it at the window, but all the rocks were covered with snow.

Who the heck was the bald guy? He might be a criminal of some sort. He had the face for crime—beat-up and mean. He had the build for crime—husky and muscle-bound. He also seemed about as dumb as most criminals are. Staring at Hogan's uniform jacket was about the stupidest move I'd ever seen.

And who were the guys in city clothes? Why had they ducked their heads?

I stared at the cars in the visitor spots. It was easy to match them with the visitors inside Hogan's office. The flashy SUV went with the ugly fellow, and the nondescript Buick with the guys in city coats. Both vehicles, I noted, had Illinois tags.

I considered throwing a rock at one of the cars, too, but instead I stomped all the way back to the shop, getting angrier with each stomp. I was completely oblivious to what was going on around me. If there had been any traffic in downtown Warner Pier at six thirty on a February evening, I might have walked in front of a truck. Luckily, the only vehicle that passed was some supersized SUV. I stepped right in front of it, but the monster paused to give me the right of way.

I could simply have murdered Joe. His mother didn't want *me* at this big family meeting. In-laws were invited as a courtesy. Mercy and Mike wanted to talk to Joe and Tony, their sons.

How could Joe do this to me? How could he do it to his mother?

But Joe understood the whole situation, I reminded myself. If he couldn't leave the meeting in Hogan's office, it must be something important. But what was more important than his mother's plans for her life?

I was still mad when I got into my van. I slammed the door so hard I nearly broke the window out. I turned on the ignition and gunned the motor loudly. I shot out of my parking place.

What was I going to tell Mercy?

When I got to the corner I turned toward Dock Street, the most direct route to Mercy's house. I automatically checked out the spot where the Georgia vehicle had been parked. At least that car had moved.

As I went by the end of our alley, I glanced down it, toward the shop. And there, under the light over our back door, I saw Aunt Nettie's blue Buick.

Oh, yikes! Aunt Nettie was back at the shop. Was something wrong?

I decided I'd better check. I threw on my brakes, backed up ten feet, then turned into the alley. I drove slowly. Aunt Nettie's car was square in my headlights.

And so, I realized, was Aunt Nettie herself. She was at the back door of the shop, fumbling with the door. As I watched she shoved at it frantically. But it didn't open.

I stopped about twenty feet away, opened my door, and stepped out.

"Aunt Nettie? What's up?"

"Lee!"

"Yes, it's me. Did I frighten you?"

"I hardly know."

Aunt Nettie was squinting in the headlights, and I saw that she was holding something. A bottle. She had it by the neck, and she was holding it upside down, almost as if she was ready to use it as a club.

"I was just checking to see if anything was wrong," I said.

Aunt Nettie made a sound I can only describe as a hysterical giggle. "Wrong?" She giggled again. "Oh, what could be wrong?"

"Well, you're standing there holding that bottle as if you're ready to attack."

"It's too late for an attack." Aunt Nettie used the bottle to point with. "Look!"

I followed the line of the bottle. There, wedged between our Dumpster and the wall, was a lump. A large lump.

And it was a lump outlined with what looked like polyester fur.

I edged toward the mass. It was a person. A man was lying on the icy asphalt of our alley.

My nerves jumped all over. "Oh, no! I'll call an ambulance!"

"I think he's beyond an ambulance," Aunt Nettie said. "I think he's dead."

I ran back to the van, grabbed my cell phone, and called 9-1-1. Aunt Nettie stood silently as I told the dispatcher about finding the man in the alley. She said she'd have the Warner Pier patrol car there within minutes.

"Please page Chief Jones," I said. "He'll want to know. His wife found the man."

"Do you recognize him?" she asked.

"Recognize him?" I repeated the words. "I haven't looked that closely."

Aunt Nettie spoke then. "It's that detective," she said. "That one who came looking for Pamela."

Then she dropped the bottle. It shattered into big shards of glass.

Chapter 3

I almost dropped the cell phone. "Derrick Valentine?"

"I didn't know his name."

I went over to the figure on the ground. The man was stuffed behind the trash container. I remember thinking that it would have taken a strong person to get him into the tight space. Then I realized the Dumpster was on wheels. It would have been simple to shove him against the wall, then move the Dumpster in front of him. Well, fairly easy. The Dumpster was pretty full, but it wasn't an especially large Dumpster, and most of our trash is cardboard and plastic.

Aunt Nettie stood there shaking, and I stayed on the line with the dispatcher until the patrol car came. Within seconds Hogan showed up, too. Joe was with him.

When Hogan arrived, Aunt Nettie began to sniffle and her story tumbled out. After she got home from work, Hogan had called to tell her he wouldn't be in until quite late. So she decided to go back to the shop and mix some Amaretto filling.

"Lee got us a new bottle of Amaretto this afternoon," she said, her voice breaking. "I thought I'd make some so the ladies could get started on a new batch of truffles first thing in the morning."

Aunt Nettie had eaten a quick supper, then driven to the shop and parked in her regular spot, under the big light over our alley door.

The first sign that something wasn't right came as she walked up to the door and almost stepped on an empty bottle. Since Aunt Nettie is naturally neat, even in an alley, she picked it up.

"It was the empty Amaretto bottle we had thrown out this afternoon! I couldn't see how it got out of the trash. So I started to put it back."

That was when she saw the man behind the Dumpster.

She had first thought he was drunk and passed out, as I had thought, but when she looked more closely she saw blood. Then she saw the odd polyester fur around his hood, and she got a glimpse of his face. She recognized him as the man who had been in the shop that afternoon.

Aunt Nettie doesn't carry a cell phone. She tried to get into the shop to call the police, but she was so upset she hadn't been able to get her key in the lock. She had still been fumbling when I drove up.

Hogan was hugging her. "You didn't know the guy's name?"

"Lee talked to him. She said he was a private detective. He was looking for someone." She pulled away from Hogan and looked at me. The floodlights the patrolman was setting up reflected in her eyes, making them look like red spotlights, and for a moment she looked like a madwoman.

"But we didn't know anything"—she repeated the word—"*anything* about that woman."

She had given me my instructions. I wasn't to mention Pamela.

So I didn't. I opened the back door that had given Aunt Nettie trouble, led Hogan, Aunt Nettie, and Joe through to the office, and found Derrick Valentine's business card. I had to think for a few minutes, but I came up with the name of the woman he'd been looking for. I hadn't written it down.

"Christina Meachum," I told Hogan. "We have no one working here by that name. And I haven't had an application from anyone named Meachum."

I was relieved that Hogan didn't ask any more, such as, "Did he show you a picture?" Or, "Had you seen the woman in the picture?" I hate quibblers, people who lie by omission or by answering only part of the question. But what else could I do? Aunt Nettie obviously didn't think we should blow Pamela's cover. So I was relieved when Hogan kept things superficial. I knew he wouldn't always. The next day's questions would be more searching, and he was sure to catch on if either of us tried evading them.

By then Hogan had called the Michigan State Police, the agency that helps small municipalities with criminal investigations, and asked for the crime scene crew. His off-duty patrolmen—both of them—arrived, and he sent one of them out to the local motel, the only one open that winter, to find out if Derrick Valentine had been registered. The routine business of crime investigation was under way.

Neither Hogan nor Joe made any reference to the conference in Hogan's office, but Hogan seemed to consider Valentine's death as a personal inconvenience rather than a major crime. Or that was what I concluded when I heard him mutter to Joe. "At least the FBI's not involved in this," he said.

Joe kept an eye on Aunt Nettie and me in the office. I made him call his mother to tell her we wouldn't be there for dinner.

As an excuse for missing a dinner engagement, finding a dead body is way better than saying you have to work late, and Joe shamelessly used Derrick Valentine's demise. I got mad at him all over again, but this wasn't the time to yell.

The most embarrassing part was that Joe's mom was so darn understanding. She said she and Mike would have us all for dinner the next day instead. She asked to talk to me. "I'm so sorry you and Nettie had this terrible experience," she said. "Let me know if there's anything I can do. Anything at all. And if dinner tomorrow won't work, we'll do it the first time you and Joe can get free."

I felt like a worm, and I hoped Joe did, too.

Joe, Aunt Nettie, and I stayed in the office about an hour, until Hogan told us we could go. Hogan said he'd get Nettie's car home after the crime scene people had looked things over. So I drove her home in my van, with Joe following in his truck.

It was the first time Aunt Nettie and I had been alone to talk, and we talked hard.

"We've got to tell Hogan that Derrick Valentine was looking for Pamela," I said.

"I know, Lee. But we don't have to tell him about it tonight."

"It could be important. Vital."

"I know." Aunt Nettie's voice was miserable. "I'll call Sarajane as soon as we get to my house."

"Even if Sarajane thinks we shouldn't tell, we have to do it anyway."

"I know, I know! But I just feel that we have to give Pamela a chance. She's in so much danger, Lee. You don't know all she's been through. We can wait until tomorrow. Please."

I can't say no to Aunt Nettie. She's closer to me than my mother. And she's a smart lady. I trust her judgment. Also, for the first time I realized that Sarajane had told her things about Pamela's situation that neither of them had told me. I knew I couldn't point Pamela out until Aunt Nettie said it was okay.

When we got to Aunt Nettie's house, she hung her coat up, then excused herself and went into the bathroom. Joe didn't seem to notice that she took the cordless telephone with her.

Alone with Joe, I decided to go on the attack. Not only was I mad at Joe over the way he'd deliberately misled his mom, I wanted to cover any sounds from Aunt Nettie's conversation with Sarajane.

I folded my arms and faced Joe. "So. Who were those guys you and Hogan were talking to? And why was that conversation going to take you until midnight?"

"You haven't told anybody about seeing them?"

"No. You said not to. Besides, Aunt Nettie is the only person I've seen since you tossed me out of the police department and closed the Venetian blind in my face. And when I saw her we were standing over a dead body. That seemed to be a more important topic of conversation than some hulking strangers in Hogan's office."

Joe put his arms around me. I kept my arms folded. We were nose to nose. He didn't have the nerve to kiss me.

"Lee, I can understand why you want an explanation."

"Oh?"

"And I could come up with one."

"And?"

"And it would be a lie."

"A lie!"

"Yes. You and I have very few secrets from each other. But the matter under discussion tonight . . ."

"Now you sound like a lawyer."

"I'm supposed to. The matter under discussion tonight was confidential to the nth degree. I cannot tell you what was going on."

"It was obviously important."

"No comment."

I unfolded my arms and slid them around him. I moved my body against his, batting my eyes in a parody of seductiveness. "There's no way I can convince you that you should tell me?"

"If you keep that up, you might. But then—as the cliché goes—I'd have to kill you. So I'd rather you didn't unleash your powers on me. I like having you around."

"Okay. I guess I can accept that. But I'm not sure I like your leading your mom astray."

"When did I do that?"

"When you told her the reason you couldn't come over tonight was because Aunt Nettie and I found that dead guy."

"That was the reason."

"*A* reason. Not *the* reason."

"The body was a reason. The City Hall emergency was also a reason, true, but if I can't explain it to you, I can't explain it to my mom either. So it's smarter not to bring it up."

He kissed me. I kissed him back.

He whispered in my ear, "Please don't rat me out, okay?"

"Will you explain as soon as you can?"

"Oh, yeah. Gladly." He kissed me again.

At that moment, the phone calls began.

The first one was from Lindy. She called my cell phone. I heard it, far off in my purse in the other room, and barely got the phone out before it told her to leave a message.

"Lee!" She sounded excited. "Are you okay?"

"Sure. Joe and I brought Aunt Nettie home. She was pretty shocked at finding a body at the back door of the shop."

"Hogan said it was some guy from out of town."

"That's right, but when did you talk to Hogan?"

"Mike called him."

"Oh." I hadn't thought about it, but I guess the mayor needs the police chief's cell phone number.

"Hogan made him sound like some garden-variety druggie, but it's not fun for something like that to happen at your back door."

Garden-variety druggie? Hogan had said that? Hmmm. That wasn't my impression. But before I could decide how to reply, Lindy went on. "Anyway, it'll get Warner Pier's mind off the return of the Prodigal guy."

"The prodigal guy? Who are you talking about?"

"You know. That guy who's CEO of Prodigal Corporation. The one who's been all over the news, thanks to the big SEC probe."

"Marson Endicott?"

"That's the one. He's apparently coming back."

"Back? Is he from Warner Pier?"

"No. He's a summer person. He owns that big house that looks like Monticello with three domes. The one everybody calls 'the Dome Home.'"

"I didn't know that was his."

"Endicott built the house about five years ago, but he's only been here one summer. It's mostly been leased."

Lindy would have gone on, but Aunt Nettie's regular phone rang.

I seized the excuse to hang up. "Lindy, there's another call. I'll talk to you later."

I took the second call on the living room phone. It was the man who owns the wine shop next door to TenHuis Chocolade. "I was coming home by way of Peach Street, and something was going on in our alley. I wondered if Hogan could tell me what happened."

I knew it was the first of a dozen such calls. Luckily, Hogan and Aunt Nettie had caller ID, so I decided not to answer any more unless they came from Hogan.

But the telephone had rung, so I deduced that Aunt Nettie had finished talking to Sarajane. Sure enough, she came out from the bedroom and smiled sweetly. "You two can go home now. Sarajane is coming over to stay with me for a while."

Joe made a few objections, but Aunt Nettie was determined. I understood that she and Sarajane wanted a heart-to-heart chat.

As we left I was able to whisper to her, "Lay down the law to Sarajane. A murder investigation takes precedence over her underground railroad."

Aunt Nettie smiled sweetly again. She didn't argue, but she didn't agree either.

There was a plot to subvert the law—right in the home of the police chief. And the plotter was a law-abiding person like my aunt Nettie. What next?

Joe was waiting beside my van. "Do you want to get a pizza?"

Suddenly I was starving. We went to the Dock Street Pizza Place, hid out at a back booth, drank beer, and ate a large pepperoni. Only a few people spoke to us.

One, oddly enough, was Frank Waterloo. I found Frank's contact unexpected, because we're not close friends. Joe and I had met him a couple of years earlier when his brother-in-law had a public run-in with Joe, then was found murdered. The killer is today in prison, but it was an unpleasant episode in our lives and in the lives of Frank Waterloo and his wife. When we see one another these days, we all four tend to nod distantly and go our own ways. Now I looked up to see Frank standing beside our booth. He looked slightly balder and slightly wider in girth than the last time I'd seen him.

"Hi, Joe," he said. "I just wondered if Mike is planning to run for mayor again."

"I hope so," Joe said. "I like his ten-year plan, and I'd like to see him oversee at least its beginning."

Frank smiled more widely. "I guess it would be to your advantage if he hangs in there."

Joe's answer was noncommittal. "We work together well."

Frank gave a chuckle. It wasn't a pleasant sound. Then he walked toward the door.

"What was all that about?" I said.

"Possibly about me becoming the mayor's stepson," Joe said. "It also probably means Frank's pal Wallace Egan is planning to run against Mike."

"For the second time?"

"Third," Joe said. "Forget it. Let's get a to-go box for the leftovers and head home."

Joe and I live across the bridge over the Warner River. Our

road, Lake Shore Drive, parallels the shore of Lake Michigan. Every town, village, and city on Lake Michigan has either a Lake Shore Drive or a Lakeshore Drive.

We live in the old TenHuis house, a Midwestern farmhouse-style home originally built by my great-grandfather as a summer cottage. Our neighborhood is about two-thirds summer cottages and one-third year-round homes.

Lake Shore Drive has houses on both sides. Most of the lots are larger than regular city lots, and the area is heavily wooded, so it has a rural feel. When the neighborhood's population takes its winter drop, we might as well live way out in the country. So I noticed when a car pulled out of our driveway onto Lake Shore Drive.

That driveway serves only our house. There is a cut-through to one neighboring house, true, but we don't pay our snowplow man to keep the cut-through open. So if someone was pulling out of our drive in February, that someone had been to our house.

I wasn't in the mood for company, and I was glad we'd missed whoever it was. I passed the car—it was too dark to get a good look at it—and turned into the drive. Joe's truck, with his VINTAGE BOATS logo on its door, was right behind me.

We went around the house and parked side by side in the drive. But we hadn't reached the back door—we always go in the back door—before lights flashed on the trees. I realized that a car was coming up the drive.

Joe stopped. "Were you expecting someone?"

"Not me. It's probably someone who wants to know all about the body in the alley."

"Go on inside," Joe said. "I'll head 'em off."

I unlocked the door and went in. I'd barely hung my coat

on the rack near the back door when I heard voices approaching.

Drat. Joe was bringing someone in.

The storm door opened. "Lee, we have a visitor," Joe said.

I didn't say anything, but I tried to put a welcoming look on my face.

A tall, distinguished-looking man came in. He wore a beautiful flannel overcoat, not unlike the ones the guys in Hogan's office had been wearing. He had a furry hat, and a scarf I was willing to bet was cashmere was tucked inside his collar.

He pulled off his leather gloves and held out a large, broad hand.

I guess I held my hand out, too, because he took it.

"Sorry to come by so late," he said. "I'm a voice from Joe's past."

Chapter 4

Joe's smile looked welcoming. I was the only person who might have guessed that it was not his best, tip-top, A1, glad-to-see-you smile.

"Lee, this is Marty Ludlum," he said. "He was a member of Clementine's firm when I was working there."

"Hello, Marty."

Marty grinned an impish grin, a grin a jury might find entrancing. "Sorry to drop by so late," he said, "but when I saw you two pulling into the drive, I couldn't resist."

Joe took his coat. I mouthed the word "Coffee?" behind the visitor's back, and Joe picked up the cue. "You still a major coffee drinker, Marty?"

"Oh, I don't want to put you out."

We went through the usual routine. "It's not late. Do you drink decaf?" "Anything." "We have both." "Regular, please." Then Joe motioned the man toward the living room, and I reached for the coffeepot.

Joe's invitation intrigued me. He obviously wanted to be friendly to Marty Ludlum, but he didn't seem entirely whole-hearted about it. Joe didn't have many good things to say about his time at "Clementine's firm." What was his relationship with this guy? Plus, it was nearly ten o'clock, a little late for a coffee klatch. If a former professional associate showed up in the driveway at that time of night, Joe could have arranged to meet him for lunch the next day. Why had Joe asked him in? The whole episode was mysterious.

"Clementine" was Joe's first wife, Clementine Ripley, who had been one of the most prominent defense attorneys in the United States. When Joe had met her, he was a young lawyer working for a nonprofit legal assistance agency in Detroit. He approached her for advice about a client he was convinced was innocent, and she agreed to take the case pro bono. The cynical side of me believes she was more attracted by the handsome young lawyer who revered her legal skills than she was by the innocent client. At any rate, before the case came to trial she and Joe had eloped to Las Vegas.

Being fifteen years younger than Clementine meant he had walked into a situation that drew more jokes than good wishes from friends, business associates, and gossipmongers. In addition to the age difference, Clementine was famous, and Joe wasn't. Their unlikely romance became fodder for the nation's tabloids.

I think Joe and Clementine did try to make their unconventional marriage work. Joe quit his Detroit job and moved to Chicago, Clementine's center of operations. He took a job as a public defender there. That caused them problems. So he became an attorney in Clementine's firm. That caused them a different set of problems. More and more frequently Joe discovered that he disagreed with Clementine's ideas on legal ethics. He isn't the type of man who hides his opinions. The marriage turned from joke to disaster.

After five years Joe gave up—not only on his marriage to

Clementine, but also on the practice of law. He moved back home to Warner Pier, bought a boat restoration business, and filed for divorce. It was four years before he put a finger back in the legal pie and took a part-time job as city attorney for his hometown, the job he was now planning to resign.

Joe came out of the experience with a very cynical view of big defense lawyers, and Marty Ludlum was apparently a partner in such a firm. So I was back to my first question. Why had Joe invited him in for a cup of coffee?

I could hear Joe and Marty's conversation in the living room, and it all seemed to be along the line of "whatever happened to old so-and-so?" Then I heard Joe say, "I'll see if Lee needs any help." As he came into the kitchen, I was about to take down the carafe we used for coffee on weekends, when we had a little more leisurely breakfast.

"Need any help?" he said loudly; then he whispered, "Don't leave me alone with Marty."

"Reach down the carriage," I said loudly. "I mean, the carafe! The stainless-steel one." Then I whispered, "Why not?"

Joe clanked the stainless-steel carafe as he pulled it off the top shelf—a shelf I can reach perfectly well. "I'll tell you later." He was still whispering.

"You can take the coffee mugs out to the living room," I said aloud. I whispered, "Don't mention that Aunt Nettie and I found a body. I don't want to talk about it."

Joe nodded.

"And tell Marty we don't stock cream," I said in a normal voice. "Just two percent."

"Sure," Joe said; then he whispered, "And for God's sake don't ask Marty why he came!" He scooped up the three coffee mugs and three napkins I'd already put out on the counter and went back to the living room.

Hmmm. The situation was more mysterious than I'd realized. And the conversation might get stilted, since I didn't want to talk about finding Valentine's body and Joe didn't want to know why this man had turned up in Michigan's leading summer resort in the wintertime. Heaven knows what Marty Ludlum didn't want to talk about. We might have to fall back on politics and religion—the topics usually forbidden in polite society.

I loaded a tray with the rest of the coffee paraphernalia. By the time I'd put a few chocolates on a plate, the coffee was made. I poured it into the carafe and added that to the grouping.

Marty Ludlum beamed when I put the tray down on the coffee table. "Chocolate! My weakness." He turned to Joe. "I remember now. Somebody told me your wife is in the chocolate business."

"The bonbons have Baileys Irish Cream filling," I said. "I confess they came home free because they were accidentally decorated to look as if they had crème de menthe filling. And the dark chocolate cupids didn't come out of the mold right. The design on top is messy. So you're getting TenHuis Chocolade seconds, but they ought to taste okay."

"They look good to me!" Marty Ludlum enthusiastically bit a bonbon. "Great! Worth a trip to rural Michigan in the dead of winter."

"Are you a summer person?"

He blinked. "I don't like really hot weather," he said.

I realized how dumb my question had sounded, and I made the mistake of trying to explain it. " 'Summer people' is the term we Warner Pier locals use for people who own cottages or who lease places here every summer. I guess I was asking if this is your first trip to Warner Pier."

"It isn't my first trip, but I'm not a regular visitor."

"Then I'm surprised you found us. This part of Warner Pier is rather obscure."

Marty Ludlum's eyes focused on his coffee cup. "I used to stay with someone who rented a cottage on Lake Shore Drive."

Joe smiled. "Lee knows that Clementine used to lease a cottage about a quarter of a mile from here, Marty."

"Oh, yes," I said. "Before she built Warner Point she stayed in the Lally house. Joe told me she used to hold conferences on her cases there."

Ludlum relaxed a bit. I made hostess noises, being careful not to ask why he had come to Warner Pier, as Joe had requested. And I didn't leave Joe alone with him.

The conversation went back to whatever-happened-to questions. I was surprised that Joe was able to ask about so many people. In fact, every time Marty tried to change the direction of the conversation, Joe seemed to think of another person he wanted to know about. That was interesting.

We drank our coffee. I stayed planted at the end of the couch, listening and asking the occasional question. When Joe ran out of people to ask about, I quizzed Marty about his family. He was divorced, he said. No kids. He had an apartment in Chicago, right off the Loop.

In exchange Marty asked me about TenHuis Chocolade. I explained that I did everything there except make chocolate. "I keep the books, order supplies, pay the taxes, process the orders—even make deliveries if there's nobody else around to do it."

After thirty minutes I guess it became obvious to Marty that I wasn't going to leave so that he and Joe could have a private chitchat. He leaned back in his chair and turned to Joe. "Maybe you've picked the best life, Joe. Nice wife, quiet town, comfortable house, no pressure to snag the big cases." Was I imagining condescension in his voice?

Joe shrugged. "I'm Warner Pier city attorney, you know. They only pay me for one day a week, but I assure you small towns are not without their own kind of pressure. When everybody knows everybody else, feelings can run pretty high. Plus, the boat shop is my major occupation, and boat owners can be pushy, too."

"Do you ever miss the firm?"

"Do I miss the high-pressure life? I never really knew it, Marty. I was always an outsider. I just watched Clementine take tranquilizers; I never took any myself." He took a drink of coffee. "I've had some offers from Michigan firms. But I've never been tempted to accept one of them."

"Never?"

Joe grinned. "If the offers begin to sound good, I go varnish a hull and realize how much better off I am."

Marty looked at me. "This guy! One of the best cross-examiners I ever watched work. How about you, Lee? Wouldn't you like a husband who was tops in his profession?"

"I have one," I said. "The boats Joe restores are works of art."

Marty smiled. "Yes, but—"

I cut him off. "And if you're talking about the financial

rewards—well, I do Joe's taxes, and he's doing okay money-wise." We're doing okay as long as we follow our budget; I didn't say that part out loud. "We're making it fine."

"Fine? Joe should be financially amazing!"

"Once I had a husband who was financially amazing. Once was enough."

Marty looked surprised, and Joe laughed. "Give it up, Marty. Lee and I have both tried the high life. We're happy in our rut. We like Warner Pier."

"Okay! I give up. You're not coming back to the old firm." Marty sipped his coffee, put down his cup, and leaned toward Joe. "So, how about a little consulting work?"

Joe didn't hesitate before he spoke.

"No," he said.

"Not even providing a little local knowledge?"

"Nope."

Marty chuckled and got to his feet. He held out his large hand to me again. "Lee, you make great coffee, and your company makes great chocolates. Thanks for both. And, Joe, it's been super seeing you."

After he had put on his coat, Marty gave Joe a handshake and one of those combined stomach bumps and back pats that men substitute for a kiss on the cheek. I decided I didn't have to follow the two of them out to Marty's car. Surely Joe's instruction not to leave them alone didn't mean I had to tramp outside in the snow. I did stand on the back porch and watch until Marty drove off. He didn't dawdle. If he told Joe any unwitnessed secrets, he did it fast.

Joe waved at the retreating car, then came back up the walk. As soon as he was inside the kitchen, I turned out the porch light and locked the door.

"And now," I said, "what the heck was that all about?"

"Just a friendly call from an old business associate."

"Oh, sure. An old friend you've never mentioned before. A friendly visit I was instructed not to ask questions about."

Joe was looking slightly amused. "You're pretty good at deductions, Lee. What have you figured out?"

"First, you knew why he was here, and you didn't want to talk about it."

"Got it."

"And he wanted to influence you about whatever it was. So he offered you a little consulting work."

Joe reacted by going into the living room and beginning to load mugs onto the tray. I followed him and picked up the carafe.

"So it's something that affects the Village of Warner Pier."

Joe didn't respond.

I went on. "But I don't see how it can be, unless the council is planning to sue somebody."

"Why do you say that?"

"Because I'm assuming Marty Ludlum is a defense attorney. A high-priced defense attorney. I can't even think of anybody who would be in Warner Pier in the wintertime who could afford him."

Then I gasped.

Joe looked at me sharply. "What?"

"Is he representing Marson Endicott?"

Joe lost his poker face. His eyes widened. Then he rolled them. He laughed, but the laughter had a hollow sound.

"How'd you come up with Marson Endicott?" he said.

"Lindy mentioned him when she called earlier. I guess the Dome Home has been opened—right in the middle of winter.

She seemed to think that was more interesting than Aunt Nettie finding a body in our alley."

Joe picked up the tray. He'd regained control of his face
and was once more Mr. Deadpan. "I guess Marson Endicott
could afford a legal team that would include Marty Ludlum,"
he said.

Then he walked to the kitchen, with me trailing along
carrying the carafe. "If I were Marty Ludlum I'd want my
money up front," I said. "Judging by what I read in *Time*
magazine."

"I assure you Marty knows how to get his fees paid."

"But why would you care?"

"When I was doing my miserable time at Clementine's
firm, Marty was one of the few people who were nice to me. I
wouldn't like to see him lose a legitimate fee."

"I mean why would you care about the Endicott case?
Whatever happens to Endicott—or to Marty Ludlum—would
it be any skin off your nose?"

"Nope." Joe put the tray down on the kitchen counter.
"We've missed the eleven o'clock news. I think I'll get ready
for bed."

"Joe!"

"What?"

"You haven't told me why you didn't want to be alone
with Marty Ludlum."

"No, I haven't, have I? So if anybody asks, you don't know
a thing."

He kissed my cheek. Then he went into the bedroom.

I stood in the kitchen and seethed.

Joe and I didn't usually have secrets from each other. And
now—twice in the same evening—he had refused to tell me

what was going on. First he wouldn't tell me about the big guys who had been in Hogan's office. And now he wouldn't explain what was going on with Marty Ludlum.

I could handle it two ways, I decided. I could scream and yell and demand that he tell me. Or I could respect his reticence.

After all, I wasn't entirely innocent when it came to keeping secrets. Aunt Nettie and I were keeping mum about Pamela, about her being in the shop when the dead detective, Derrick Valentine, came looking for her. True, Aunt Nettie had promised to tell Hogan tomorrow, but so far she and I were keeping it a secret.

But our secret was for a good reason, I told myself self-righteously. We had a good reason. We were trying to protect Pamela.

Maybe Joe had a good reason, too.

I decided that respecting Joe's reticence might be the best way to handle the situation. I wouldn't ask, or even hint that I wanted to know. I wouldn't sulk or beg.

Then maybe he'd tell me anyway.

As I heard Joe go into the bathroom, I felt smug. I had my self-righteousness back.

I was hugging it to myself and loading coffee mugs into the dishwasher when someone rapped softly at the back door.

After my heart started beating again, I heard Aunt Nettie's voice. "Lee! Lee, let us in!"

At least it sounded like Aunt Nettie. But how could Aunt Nettie be here? If she was coming over—at eleven thirty at night—surely she would call first.

I guess no one could blame me for being a little cautious. The logical part of my brain told me to fling the back door open for Aunt Nettie. But all I could think of was Derrick Valentine lying dead behind the Dumpster.

There was a chain on that back door, and I left it hooked when I turned the handle.

Aunt Nettie stood on the porch. Her blond-white hair was covered with a funny knit cap she wears when it's really cold; only a few curls were sticking out. Her face was worried.

"Lee, please let us in."

I unhooked the chain and opened the door. "Come in! But who is 'us'?"

Aunt Nettie slipped into the kitchen, then turned and looked behind her. "Come on," she said. "Come on in. This is the safest place I can think of."

The light from the kitchen threw of patch of glitter on the snow. All was quiet outside. Then I saw movement. Slowly Pamela walked into the light and up the steps onto the back porch.

Chocolate Chat
Speaking Chocolate

Like all specialized fields, chocolate growing and production has its own vocabulary. Reading about chocolate means conquering words such as "conching," "bakjes," and "bloom."

Not to mention "cacao" and "cocoa."

"Cacao" is the plant that produces chocolate. The cacao tree originally came from Central and South America, and today is also cultivated in Africa, Southeast Asia, Hawaii, and the West Indies. Its seeds are "cocoa beans," with thirty or forty beans found inside large seed pods that grow on the trunks of the trees. The beans are surrounded by a sweet pulp that probably originally drew people to the beans.

After procedures that include fermenting, drying, cleaning, roasting, winnowing, blending, refining, conching, tempering, molding—and others—the beans become cocoa or chocolate.

"Cocoa" usually refers to that dry powder used to make a hot, yummy chocolate drink or in recipes. It may be either "Dutched" or "natural." Dutched cocoa has been treated with an alkali to neutralize some of the acidity of chocolate. It is darker in color than natural cocoa, but has a milder flavor. If a recipe specifies one kind or the other, do not substitute.

Chapter 5

Pamela looked so sheepish I expected her to bleat. So it was startling when she started her first sentence with "baa."

"Baaad penny," she said. "I keep turning up. You'll never get rid of me."

"I wouldn't want to get rid of you, except that we want you to be safe." They came inside, and I closed the door behind the two of them. "What's happened?"

Aunt Nettie dropped the duffel bag she was carrying and pulled her funny cap off. "Where's Joe?"

"In the shower."

"Good!" She turned to Pamela. "The shower in this house hides all other sounds. We can get you upstairs and Joe won't know you're here."

"Aunt Nettie! We can't do that!"

Aunt Nettie gave me a questioning look. "No?"

"No! For one thing, this is Joe's home. I'm not going to have things going on here that he doesn't know about."

Aunt Nettie grimaced. "I guess it would be pretty sneaky."

"It certainly would be. Besides, it's not practical." Now I turned to Pamela. "We can't keep the shower going twenty-four hours a day. And this house is like an amplifier. Drop a pin in the kitchen, and people in the bedroom hear it land. If we tried to hide you upstairs—well, we could wrap you up like a mummy, and Joe would still hear the floor creak."

"I told Nettie that I've caused you both enough trouble," Pamela said. "I feel simply terrible about this. Isn't there some way I can simply get a cab and head out of town?"

"No!" Aunt Nettie was aghast. "I told you, Pamela! There are no cabs in Warner Pier. Not in winter anyway."

"I'm all confused," I said. "Why does Pamela need to leave Sarajane's?"

Aunt Nettie and Pamela exchanged looks. Pamela spoke. "I got a threatening phone call."

"Oh," I said. A threatening phone call to Sarajane's B&B meant that someone had traced Pamela there. And, yes, that meant she had to find a new hiding place.

"When Sarajane got home from my house," Aunt Nettie said, "she found Pamela trying to call a cab. Of course, this time of year we'd have to get one from Holland. So Sarajane called me. We arranged to meet at that Gulf station out on the highway. It stays open all night. I got Pamela away out the back door."

She took a deep breath. "I thought you might be able to hide her overnight. Where else can I take her?"

I made a snap decision. "This is as good as anyplace. Come on." I picked up Pamela's duffel bag and headed for the stairs.

"But it's dangerous to have me around!" Pamela sounded plaintive. "If Harold finds me, he may—blow the house up or something. I don't want to put anyone else in danger. If I cause you or Nettie or Sarajane to get hurt—I'd never forgive myself."

"We won't let anyone in."

"If I only had a car . . . I'd drive off and never stop." Pamela looked furious.

"I understand how you feel, but I think our house had better be your stopping place for tonight."

"But what about Joe?"

"I'll tell him the truth. And that truth is that one of the women who works at the shop is having family problems and needs a place to stay for a couple of days."

Pamela gave a derisive snort. "I guess that's not lying."

"It's quibbling. But we can't help that." I led the way up the stairs. "Luckily, Joe put in a bathroom up here last summer, and all the beds are made."

Aunt Nettie and I deposited Pamela in the east bedroom, on the side of the house away from the road. At least the neighbors could drive down Lake Shore Drive—which was on the west side of our property—without seeing a light up there and calling to ask if we had company. Besides, the room had light-blocking shades, put up to keep out the morning sun in the summertime, so I hoped that the bedside lamp wouldn't be visible from outside at all.

"Actually, Joe doesn't know your name, so I suppose it won't matter if he does see you," I said.

"No!" Pamela's answer was sharp. Then she shook her head. "I mean, the fewer people I have contact with, the better."

"Then I'm afraid you'd better wait until Joe leaves for work before you come down for breakfast," I said. "I'll try to bring some coffee up earlier, if you like."

"That sounds wonderful. You're a perfect hostess."

Pamela sat on the edge of the bed and pulled her ever-present M&M Minis out of her jacket pocket. Then she dropped her face to her hands. She looked as if she was hanging on by one torn fingernail. I felt terribly sorry for her.

"I just can't believe the way this day has gone," she said. "It's like a door slammer."

"Buck up. We're going to make it yet." That was what I said. What I thought is a different matter. Pamela's situation looked pretty bleak.

I checked the towel and soap situation in the bathroom, then followed Aunt Nettie down the narrow stairs. At the bottom she took my arm and whispered, "What did she mean by 'a door slammer'?"

"It's a theater term. Or at least I've heard it used to refer to a type of play. The sort where people are running in and out of doors, slamming them, and winding up in the wrong bedrooms. A farce."

"I'd call today more of a tragedy." Aunt Nettie pulled on her woolly hat, and I watched from the door to make sure she got into her car safely.

I agreed with Aunt Nettie, I decided. We'd had a lot of excitement that day. And, yes, it had involved running from one place to another, disguises, ducking out doors, and hiding in strange places. The excitement had even continued after I got home, with the unexpected appearance of Joe's former business associate. But I wouldn't call the day a farce. Anything with a dead man wouldn't qualify as a farce.

I spoke aloud. "I'd call it a complete mess."

"What is?"

I jumped. Then I realized that Joe was out of the shower. He'd walked into the kitchen wearing his flannel pajamas, his hair still wet. "What's a mess?" he said.

"We've got an unexpected visitor, and her life's a mess." I gave him an expurgated version of Pamela's arrival.

Joe frowned. "Shouldn't she go to the women's shelter in Holland?"

"Probably. But Aunt Nettie thought we could take her in here tonight. She's sure her husband won't find her here."

"I'll be careful to lock up." Joe and I looked at each other wordlessly. Our hundred-year-old house simply wasn't all that secure. If somebody wanted in badly enough, they could get in.

"I'm going to bed," I said.

"It's been a long day," Joe said. "And you and Nettie are going to have to make statements tomorrow."

Only one thing was certain, I told myself as I brushed my teeth. Pamela was leaving the next day. Leaving our house, leaving Warner Pier. As far as I was concerned, she was leaving my life forever.

And if Aunt Nettie was tempted to help Sarajane with her underground railroad again—well, I'd remind her about this "door slammer."

I put on my flannel nightgown—that doesn't sound sexy, but Joe says it's soft and cuddly when it's on, and he knows how to take it off. Then I kissed Joe on the forehead—he was already asleep—and crawled into bed. The sight of the bloody polyester fur on Derrick Valentine's jacket swam briefly into my memory. I heard Pamela's step upstairs. Then I sank into sleep. It was going to take more than a slamming door to wake me up.

It took the telephone. Or maybe it was Joe's convulsive kick after it rang. Anyway, it sounded off, and we were both fighting to wake up by the second ring.

"What time is it?" Joe didn't sound happy.

"It's three thirty. It's got to be a wrong number."

The phone is on my side of the bed. When I answered I'm sure my "Hello" sounded as if it was echoing out of a cavern.

The voice in the phone was just above a whisper. "Lee Woodyard?"

I didn't recognize the caller. "Yes?"

"This is Myrl."

"Um?"

"I'm Sarajane's friend."

I think there was a long silence before her words sank in. "Sarajane?" Suddenly I woke up. This must be Sarajane's contact with the underground railroad.

I was careful to speak cautiously. "Yes?"

"Is your husband in the room with you?"

"Yes."

"Sarajane said she brought Pamela to you a few hours ago."

"Yes."

"I've come to pick her up."

I sat up. "Yes?"

"I'm at the Warner River bridge. How long will it take to get to your house?"

"Five minutes."

"Please get Pamela up. Do you think we can get her out without waking your husband up?"

"I can try. Do you know how to find the house?"

"I have a GPS." The line went dead.

I got out of bed.

Joe raised his head. "What is it?"

"It's Pamela. One of her friends has come to pick her up."

"I still think she should go to the shelter."

"I'll suggest that. Go back to sleep."

Joe obeyed. I put on my slippers and robe and headed upstairs.

When I knocked on Pamela's door she spoke so quickly that I figured she'd been awakened by the phone. There was an extension upstairs, but it was across the hall from her room.

Her voice was soft. "Lee?"

I opened the door a crack and told her about Myrl's call. "So you've got five minutes," I said.

Pamela gave such a deep sigh that I pushed the door open a bit more. She'd turned the bedside light on. "Are you okay?"

She yanked the covers over her head. All I could see of her were her eyes. They looked like a stranger's eyes. Lighter and a different shape. I realized I hadn't seen her without eye makeup before.

"Yes, I'm okay," she said. "I'm just not sure I'm up to another challenge."

"Do you know Myrl?"

"Oh, yes."

"Are you willing to go with her?"

"I guess I have to." She sounded regretful.

"Ready or not . . ."

"I'm afraid so."

I expected Pamela to toss the covers back, but she lay there without moving. I closed the door and started for the stairs, a bit surprised at her slow reaction. Maybe she was sleeping in the nude and didn't want to jump out of bed in front of me.

As I went into the kitchen and turned on the back porch and driveway lights, I heard movement upstairs, so I decided that Pamela was up.

The mysterious Myrl didn't get to the house in five minutes, but she made it inside of ten. She followed the clues of the lights, following the drive around the house and parking beside Joe's truck. By the time she came up the walk to the back door, Pamela was coming down the stairs. I opened the door.

Myrl was a raw-boned woman, nearly as tall as I am, with dark hair chopped short. She wore a heavy jacket and furry earmuffs. Her step was firm. She didn't look like the kind of woman who would take any guff, from an abusive husband or anybody else. If Pamela had had previous contact with Myrl, I could see why Pamela was ready to obey her summons.

"Hi, Myrl," I said. "Can I make some coffee for y'all to take with you?"

"Thanks, but I've got a thermos in the car." She stood awkwardly just inside the back door. "I hope Pamela doesn't have a bunch of stuff."

Pamela's voice answered. "I just have one duffel bag and a tote." She came into the kitchen. I was surprised to see that in spite of the short notice she had had, Pamela had found time to put on her eye makeup.

She walked up to Myrl. "I'm ready." Her voice was almost challenging.

Myrl gave a gasp so loud that I jumped. Pamela didn't jump, though. She stared at Myrl with eyes like obsidian.

I didn't understand that gasp. "Myrl? What's wrong?"

"Nothing. Nothing." Now Myrl sounded amused. "Well, Pamela, are you ready to go? May I carry your bag for you?" She was almost laughing.

I didn't understand Myrl's reaction—first surprise, and

then amusement—but I knew there was one thing I needed to make sure of. "So Sarajane knows how to get hold of you?"

"Oh, sure. But since nobody is staying at her place, she'll have no reason to call me."

"Unless the police need to question Pamela."

Myrl stopped halfway through the back door. "The police? Why would the police need to question Pamela?"

"Because that private detective who was looking for her was found dead."

"What!"

"Didn't Sarajane tell you?"

"No, she did not. All she said was that he'd come looking for Pamela, and that later Pamela had received a threatening phone call."

She glared at Pamela.

"Listen," Pamela said. "I don't know anything about the guy. Nothing about why he came looking for me. Nothing about how he wound up dead."

Myrl seemed to be turning the situation over in her mind. She stood staring at Pamela for at least thirty seconds. Then she abruptly turned toward her car. "There's no point in keeping Lee standing out here in the cold." Again her voice took a slightly sarcastic tone. "Come on, Pamela."

The two of them headed down the walk. And out of my life. Or so I hoped.

But they took their time getting into the car. I heard the car's trunk pop, and I saw its light go on. Then the two of them stood there, yammering at each other. I couldn't make out the words, but I could hear their voices. And they were both angry.

Oh, golly, I thought, is Pamela going to get mad and march back in?

As I stood there staring through the storm door, the argument seemed to last five or ten minutes. Actually, it was probably only two or three minutes before I saw the light from the trunk go out and heard its lid slam. Then the two of them got into the car. The car started, the motor ran the thirty seconds it takes to fasten seat belts, and then the car backed out.

Eager to be sure that they'd actually left, I went into the living room to watch them go down our lane. The car drove slowly past our front porch and out onto Lake Shore Drive. When Myrl put on her brakes and stopped to look both ways, I could even see the license plate. It was a Michigan plate, but I didn't notice the letters, because I'm a number person. The numbers were 812.

The car turned left onto Lake Shore Drive. Pamela and her problems were gone from my life.

I relocked the back door, turned out the outside lights, and crawled back into bed. Joe didn't stir. And neither did I until the phone rang again.

This time the clock read seven thirty. I growled before I answered, "Hello."

"Lee!"

This was someone I recognized. "Sarajane? What's wrong?"

"How did you know something's wrong?"

"Your voice. I recognize that worried sound."

"I hope nothing's wrong. Did Pamela and Myrl get off?"

"Yes. I watched them until they turned onto Lake Shore Drive."

"When was that?"

"Sometime around four a.m., I guess. Why?"

"They were supposed to drive over to Kalamazoo." Kalamazoo was about an hour away from us.

"Supposed to?" I sat up. "What happened?"

"We don't know! They never got there!"

Chapter 6

"We've got to call the police," I said.

"No! No!"

"Listen, Sarajane, if they've disappeared . . ."

"Lee, I can't believe anything has happened to them. Myrl is so—so competent."

"She seemed that way in the five minutes I talked to her. But someone needs to be looking for them."

"Believe me, Lee, someone is. Please don't do anything until I call back."

The line clicked dead. I got out of bed and headed for the shower. The phone call had roused me quicker than any alarm clock could.

After my shower I had time to go upstairs and strip Pamela's bed before I went to work. She hadn't been there long enough to get the room dirty, of course, and she'd seemed to have cleared everything out. The only item she had left behind was an odd one, however. As I yanked the sheets off the bed, a ring clunked onto the wooden floor. It was a class ring, a man's gold ring with a blue stone, and it was hanging on a chain. It looked for all the world like a high school going-steady ring.

I looked at it closely. The graduation date was twenty years earlier—which meshed with my idea of Pamela's age. The school initials were "FSC." A stylized cat's head was superimposed on the stone. The cat was snarling.

Maybe it was a college ring. Something State College? Pamela was supposedly from Ann Arbor. It certainly wasn't a University of Michigan ring.

I took the ring downstairs and put it in the pottery vase on the mantle—the place we reserve for useless junk. I didn't really expect to hear from Pamela again, but if I did, I could mail her the ring.

When I got to work our alley was blocked off with crime scene tape, so Aunt Nettie and I both parked in front of the shop. We got there at almost the same time. Hogan, she said, had come home just before she left and was now trying to get some sleep. And, yes, Sarajane had called her to say Myrl and Pamela were missing.

"I told her we need to report this to the police," I said, "but she says no."

"I think you're right. Now that I don't have to worry about bothering Hogan, I'll phone Sarajane and try to talk her into calling either Hogan or the State Police."

Aunt Nettie went into my office, closing the door for privacy. She was still on the phone with Sarajane when she motioned me in. "Sarajane says we could report Myrl and Pamela missing as a possible traffic accident, but she doesn't want us to say anything about Pamela being in danger. She thinks you might be the best person to make the report, Lee. Since they were last seen at your house."

"I'll be glad to. Does she know what kind of car they were in? I didn't get a good look."

Aunt Nettie consulted the telephone. "A gray Camry. But Sarajane doesn't know the license number."

"812."

"You know it?"

"I don't know the letters, but the numbers were 812."

I called the State Police office nearest Warner Pier, described the car and the route it would probably have taken to reach Kalamazoo. "They should have arrived hours ago," I said.

"No accidents have been reported," the officer answered. "And since the driver and passenger were competent adults, they're not considered missing."

"I know. I just keep picturing all those woods, and how easy it would be to skid off the road and not be visible to passing cars."

The State Police officer promised to alert patrol officers, asking them to watch for the Camry and for signs of an accident. I hung up, as worried as ever.

But my concern was nothing to Aunt Nettie's. She was literally wringing her hands. I decided I had to act calm, even if I didn't feel that way. Maybe it would help her cope.

"Okay!" I said. "We've done all we can for the moment."

"I know, I know. But it's such a dangerous situation. You don't know."

"No, I don't know, Aunt Nettie. Why don't you try telling me?"

I could see Aunt Nettie turn that over in her mind.

"I'm getting a little tired of operating in the dark," I said.

"I guess so." She leaned close and whispered. "Pamela's ex-husband is Harold Belcher."

I felt blank. "Who is he?"

"Maybe the Belcher case happened before you moved to

Michigan." Aunt Nettie shook her head sadly. "I'd better get the ladies started."

She left for the workroom. I turned on the computer and Googled Harold Belcher.

A few newspaper files informed me of the background. I won't go into all the details; Harold's nickname, "Belcher the Butcher," says enough.

Harold ran a car theft ring and processed stolen cars in a Detroit chop shop. Supposedly the operation was mob-connected, though this was never proved in court. Bad things happened to some of Harold's associates, but again no link to Harold himself had ever been proven.

Whenever Harold got frustrated with his job he apparently took his unhappiness out on his wife, Christina. This proved his undoing. After a beating landed Christina Belcher in the hospital with a broken jaw and other injuries, she was approached by law enforcement. The FBI was involved because the car theft ring had been moving cars across state lines. Desperate to escape her miserable life, Christina agreed to testify not only against Harold, but against his associates. Several people went to prison, Harold among them, and Christina got a divorce, then disappeared. Gossip was that she had entered the federal Witness Protection Program, although she had not fingered any major mob figures.

The trials had been held five years earlier. Now Harold's prison sentence was over—he'd been convicted only on minor charges, not for the heinous crimes the public was convinced he'd committed—and he had recently faced a second trial for his assaults on Christina. Christina had been brought back to Detroit to testify against him. Harold was convicted, but he was appealing the verdict.

Christina was supposedly guarded closely until she could be tucked back into the federal Witness Protection Program. No one had figured out how she had managed to disappear.

Her bodyguards had gotten up one morning to find her gone. Harold's involvement was suspected, but law enforcement had found no evidence against him. Christina was simply not around anymore.

I snorted knowingly. If Christina had turned to Myrl, and Myrl was as competent as she looked and as Sarajane thought, I could understand how Christina managed to get away from both the authorities and her ex-husband.

I printed out a picture of Harold, just so I'd have it for reference. He was a heavyset guy with dark, thinning hair. At least his hair had been thinning when the picture was taken six years earlier. His most eye-catching feature was a large, crooked nose, but he had a certain animal magnetism—I could see why he would be attractive to some women.

I found a few pictures of Christina as well. The first was identical to the one Derrick Valentine had flopped onto our counter. "Meachum," I learned from the *Detroit Free Press* files, was Christina's maiden name.

In another photo she looked young and pretty. Taken at some fancy party, the picture was a profile shot, showing Christina with her dark hair swept up onto the crown of her head. Her brown eyes sparkled, and in the lobe of her small, beautifully shaped ear was a pearl drop earring. A companion, head-on shot showed her sweet, heart-shaped face with a deep widow's peak, pouty lips, and pointed chin.

That pretty young Christina had turned into the haggard, haunted Pamela I knew, her face misshapen, her teeth missing, her makeup too heavy, her eyes red and watery. Harold Belcher should be sent up for life, I decided.

But at the present, Harold was out on bond, and Christina was the prisoner.

I printed out a couple of photos of Christina, and I had barely tucked them away in a file folder when the phone rang. It was Lindy.

"Hi," she said. "This is a quick business call. Though it might mean some fun, too."

"I love mixing business and pleasure. What's up?"

"You remember my mentioning that the Dome Home was being opened?"

"I remember. You thought that the infamous Marson Endicott was coming to town."

"Apparently he has arrived. I just got a call asking Herrera Catering to deliver sandwiches and soup for a dozen people at noon today."

"Make 'em pay cash."

Lindy laughed. "I will. If half the stuff I read in the paper is true, I'm not extending credit. But, Lee, I thought we might have some fun with it. I have to take the food out there. Why don't you come with me?"

I didn't answer immediately. Lindy spoke again. "Wouldn't you like to see the inside of that house?"

"Umm." I thought about it. The Endicott house was an amazing structure from the outside, and, yes, I'd like to see what was inside.

Then I thought about Marty Ludlum. Joe had refused to confirm that he was on the Endicott team, and Marty hadn't mentioned it either. But I couldn't figure out any other reason that a high-powered defense attorney like Marty would show up in Warner Pier in the dead of winter.

I needed more information. "Lindy, are you serving this lunch yourself?"

"No. Endicott has someone called a 'household manager.' He'll serve and clean up, but I'm going to go out about eleven thirty to set up. I wanted to see the layout and make sure everything's right. I think I'll be through by twelve fifteen or so. Then you and I could go by the Sidewalk Café and have lunch ourselves. We haven't had a good gossip session lately, and I need to talk to you."

I guess it was the "gossip session" part that made me say no to going out to the Dome Home ahead of time. Right at that moment, there were too many things going on in my life that I couldn't tell Lindy about—the strange men in the police station, the unexpected visit of Marty Ludlum, the disappearance of Pamela-Christina and Myrl Sawyer. I could probably keep quiet for the forty-five minutes it took to eat lunch, but not touching on the wrong subject for two hours might tax my tongue.

"I could meet you for lunch," I said, "but I just don't have time to go out to the Dome Home ahead of time. Even if it would make us the envy of Warner Pier." Yes, Warner Pier was really curious about the Endicott house. It loomed over our downtown—right across the river from our quaint business district, looking like three Monticellos.

"Aw, com'on, Lee."

I was tempted, but I kept to my plan. I agreed to meet Lindy at the Sidewalk Café after she had the Endicott luncheon under way.

After I hung up, I did one more thing before I started work. I called Sarajane and gave her a deadline.

"If you don't hear from Myrl by two o'clock," I told her, "I'm going to tell Hogan this whole story and take his advice on how to handle it."

She objected, but only halfheartedly. Even Sarajane knew the situation couldn't go on.

Then I got busy. I was in the back room, checking how much fondant we had in stock, when one of the ladies poked her head in and told me there was someone at the counter.

"Do you want me to wait on him?" she said.

"I'll do it."

The man standing at the front counter was a stranger, but something about him was familiar. I was saying, "May I help you?" before I realized what it was.

He was wearing Derrick Valentine's jacket.

It wasn't the same jacket, of course. That one, with its blood-soaked polyester fur, would be in a State Police evidence room someplace. But this one looked as if it had come off the same rack.

Except for size. Derrick Valentine had been tall and skinny. This guy was short, round, and cuddly, with wispy blond hair that almost curled. The two men had been named wrong. Valentine had been nothing like his name, but the guy wearing the identical jacket was a real live cupid.

"You Mrs. Woodyard?" His voice squeaked.

"Yes. And I'm terribly sorry about what happened to your partner."

His eyes popped just a little. "My partner?"

"I was guessing that you were working with Derrick Valentine. I'm sorry if I was wrong."

"No, you're not wrong. But how'd you know that?"

"The jackets. They're almost identical."

He fingered his jacket. "Oh. We bought jackets on our way here, just to last a week or so. But how did you know Derrick even had a partner?"

"Strangers in Warner Pier are easy to pick out in wintertime. And the PDQ offices are in Atlanta, and I saw a Georgia car parked around on Peach Street yesterday afternoon. Someone was sitting in it. Was it you? I jumped to the conclusion that Mr. Valentine wasn't working alone."

"Guess that marks me for a sucker. I thought I looked like a salesman."

"You did. I wouldn't have noticed you if it hadn't been for the license tag. But I am terribly sorry about Mr. Valentine. Had you worked together long?"

"No. Well, actually . . . we weren't close."

"How's Mrs. Valentine doing?"

"The boss had to tell her about Rick. Not me. How'd you know he had a wife?"

"He bought chocolates and said they were for her. Do they have children?"

"Nope." The man frowned. "Look, I'm supposed to be questioning you. How'd you turn the conversation around?"

"I'm from Texas. We're friendly and nosy. What did you want to ask me?"

"You found the body, right?"

"My aunt and I did. But we talked to the police. I'm not supposed to say anything about it."

"Maybe we ought to start from the beginning." The cupid-like man produced a card like the one Derrick Valentine had carried. It gave his name as Tom O'Sullivan.

"Rick Valentine came in looking for a woman we'd traced to this area of Michigan," he said.

"Christina Meachum. I told Mr. Valentine we didn't have anyone by that name working here, and no one by that name had applied for a job."

I wasn't lying. No one had applied for a job under the name of Christina Meachum. And we hadn't hired anyone to work under that name.

O'Sullivan stared into space without replying, so I spoke again. "What he didn't tell me was why you thought this woman would be at TenHuis Chocolade."

"Foe . . ." He seemed to realize he was saying something he shouldn't, and he stopped abruptly. "Confidential information," he said self-importantly.

He leaned an elbow on the counter with studied casualness. "Rick thought you were lying, you know."

"Why did he think that?"

"Because our information was good. We were sure she'd been here."

"How could you be sure?"

He smiled. I guess he tried to make it a knowing smile, but he missed the mark. Don't ask me how I knew, but I was sure he was bluffing.

I guess he expected me to start stammering from embarrassment at being accused of lying or to be angry because my truthfulness had been challenged. Instead I was fighting the impulse to laugh. He was a silly little man.

This was one time that being a giant among women was an advantage. I stood up to my full height, which was about eight inches taller than Tom O'Sullivan. I looked down at him.

"Sorry, Mr. O'Sullivan. I would need some facts before I believe that tale. Now—at TenHuis Chocolade, everyone who comes in gets a sample chocolate. What looks good to you?"

I moved along the counter, pointing to the various chocolates. "How about a raspberry cream? That's the round dark chocolate bonbon with one white dot. The interior is a soft pink, so it's popular around Valentine's Day. Or there's the Jamaican rum truffle. It's dark chocolate inside and out. Or lots of men like a coffee truffle—milk chocolate all the way through and flavored, of course, with coffee. That's the one decorated with white stripes."

I looked at him, smiling. Anytime I want to change the subject, chocolate gives me a great new topic. I used a little pair of tongs to pick up a Jamaican rum truffle and lift it out of the show case. I held it out enticingly.

Tom O'Sullivan didn't take it. He had lost his smirk and was glaring. "Look," he said. "I need that information."

"I've told you everything I can tell you," I said.

"But Rick said—"

I cut him off. "I'm not responsible for any conclusions poor Mr. Valentine drew. I couldn't tell him anything."

"But you called later and asked him to meet you! At the back door of this shop!"

Chapter 7

I stared at the detective. Then I lost my grip. On the Jamaican rum truffle, that is. The inch-tall pyramid of chocolate bounced off the showcase, flew onto the floor, and skidded toward the doorway.

Only then did I find my voice and deny his accusation. "I did not call Derrick Valentine! Did he tell you I had?"

"Yes."

"He lied! Or else he was completely mistaken. Have you told the police this?"

O'Sullivan's smirk was back. "Not yet. If you play ball . . ."

I reached for the telephone behind the cash register. "You must tell the investigating officers right away."

I had loaded the number for the police station into the phone to tease Aunt Nettie when she first began to see Hogan socially. Now I hit speed dial.

"This could be a valuable clue," I said. "The police need to know. Derrick Valentine was your partner! How could you not tell them?"

As the phone was answered at the police station, the bell on the shop's front door tinkled. When I looked around, Tom

O'Sullivan was outside and disappearing fast. And he wasn't disappearing in the direction of the police station.

He had taken to his heels. And he'd gone without a sample chocolate. That was some satisfaction, even though I'd thrown the Jamaican rum truffle in the floor. As a matter of fact, O'Sullivan had stepped on it as he went out.

Hogan wasn't at the station, of course, but I talked to one of the State Policemen who was there, reporting my whole conversation with the detective.

By the time I was through, I'd worked myself into a state of complete indignation. "I did not call Valentine and arrange to meet him in the alley," I said. "I'm furious at that report. And I want to make sure y'all are investigating why this Tom O'Sullivan would say such a thing."

The officer—I was so mad I didn't even get his name—made calming noises and said he'd tell "the lead investigators."

I hung up feeling quite triumphant. O'Sullivan was just trying it on, I told myself. Probably nobody had called Valentine. But I was scared, too, because I had to admit it made sense.

There had to be some reason Derrick Valentine had gone into the alley behind our shop. That alley wasn't exactly a tourist attraction.

And the alley wasn't on Valentine's way anywhere. I assumed that Valentine and O'Sullivan would have had rooms in the one Warner Pier motel that was open that winter, since it was cheaper and more anonymous than the few B&Bs that were open.

Even if Valentine was a fresh air and exercise fiend who was walking the half mile from there to the nearest restaurant, he would have had no reason to go down that alley in the normal way of things.

So what had he been doing in the alley behind our shop?

Of course, his killer could have forced him to walk there or killed him elsewhere and dragged the body down the alley, but it would have been a lot easier to entice Valentine to go there under his own power. So the murderer might have called him and claimed to be me.

But why would the murderer do that?

Valentine knew hardly anybody in Warner Pier. I would be one of the few people who could have called him. I was also one of the few people in Warner Pier with a Texas accent. Any dolt could have called him, talked through his or her nose, and y'all'ed a few times. Valentine probably would have trotted right over.

Right to his death.

I needed legal advice. I called Joe.

Joe was reassuring. I'd done the right thing, he told me, though O'Sullivan had probably made up the story about a phone call luring Valentine to the TenHuis alley.

"But, Joe, it does make sense," I said. "Why else would Valentine have gone there?"

"Because somebody had a gun in his back? Or maybe Valentine was planning to break into the shop. A lot of things could have happened. Don't worry."

I hung up reassured. Besides, who could have gotten the idea to impersonate me to Derrick Valentine? Almost nobody in Warner Pier knew that he and I had had contact.

Yes, the list was small. Sarajane, Aunt Nettie, Pamela, George Jenkins—though I don't think he actually knew the private detective's name. Those were the only people I'd told. I hadn't even mentioned it to Joe until after Valentine's body was found.

Of course, I had no idea whom Valentine might have told. His partner, O'Sullivan, obviously. Maybe his supervisor, down in Atlanta. Heck, he might have put it on the Internet. At any rate, I simply couldn't picture George, Aunt Nettie, or Sarajane luring Valentine to the alley and killing him. And Pamela certainly would have been determined to avoid him.

No, I decided, O'Sullivan had been lying about why Valentine had gone to the alley. I'd ratted him out to the State Police. I'd let them handle it. In fact, I'd let Hogan and the State Police handle everything. I cleaned the squished bonbon off the floor, feeling smug.

Except that I did have to make sure Sarajane told the detectives about Pamela being a passenger on the underground railway. And about Pamela and Myrl disappearing between Warner Pier and Kalamazoo. No, I couldn't simply forget what was going on, as much as I'd like to.

It's hard to work when you're feeling glum. I carried on until about eleven thirty, when the phone rang. The caller ID told me the call was from Lindy's cell phone.

I picked up the phone. "Hi. Is it time for lunch already?"

"Not yet. I just got a special request. Somebody out here has heard of the fabulous TenHuis chocolates. They want an assortment added to the luncheon buffet."

I thought about that. "Huh. That confirms my suspicion," I said.

"Which one?"

"A man named Marty Ludlum is out there, right? Big guy? Distinguished-looking?"

"There's a Mr. Marvin P. Ludlum. That description fits him. Do I need to ask his nickname?"

"No. Ludlum knows Joe. I suspected he was mixed up with Endicott." I sighed. "I'll bring the chocolates out. How many do you need?"

"We might as well soak 'em for a couple of pounds."

"I'll drop them off at the back door."

"The layout out here means you have to come to the front. There are only two parking spaces near the kitchen."

"Twenty minutes."

I hung up. Then I snarled. I couldn't refuse a request from Lindy, but I did not want to see Marty Ludlum. I didn't know why Joe wanted to avoid him, so if Marty tried to talk to me, I didn't know which questions to answer and which ones to dodge. There were too many things I couldn't mention that day; it was hard remembering which ones I couldn't mention to which people.

I took two one-pound boxes of assorted chocolates from the shelf. I was darned if the crowd at the Endicott house was going to get anything special. Then I grabbed a plastic caterer's tray—the kind with a fake silver finish—in case Lindy wanted to put them on it. I told Aunt Nettie where I was headed. In fact, I asked her if she didn't want to handle the delivery herself. She said no.

The Endicott house was on the Warner River, almost directly across from the business district. I could see it as I pulled out of my parking slot in front of TenHuis Chocolade, but I had to drive a half mile upstream, cross the bridge, and drive west a half mile to get there.

When I got to the entrance, of course, I was stopped by a wrought-iron gate and a faraway, invisible security guard who communicated electronically. The elaborately landscaped estate probably required security guards because it might as well have had a sign reading, "Fancy house filled with expensive, easy-to-fence items." But Marson Endicott's legal problems also made a high level of security advisable, if only to keep reporters out. Not that the site would have been hard to get into. The road was lined by iron fencing, true, but that fencing was designed to allow us peons to look in enviously. I speculated that an intruder could get over with the help of a small step stool and a throw rug. After all, people get into the White House grounds now and then, despite the U.S. Secret Service. Marson Endicott's security didn't match that.

The guard's electronic voice told me to drive on to the front door, and the gate slid back magically. There was, naturally, a wide circular drive. It was lined with parked cars, all expensive models. The Herrera Catering van wasn't in view, so I thought Lindy had copped one of the two kitchen parking spaces. It would have looked a bit beat-up compared to the Mercedeses, BMWs, and Lexuses. Or is that Lexi?

I drove up the drive, gawking at the house. Its exterior might have been a Monticello rip-off, but the architect had missed classic revival and settled for nouveau riche. Its bricks were a bit too red, the domes a little too ornate, the outdoor light fixtures a tad too gimcracky to look like genuine class.

I stopped in front of the central door and waited for the security guard, or someone, to come out. No one came. So I moved the van farther down and parked. I gathered up my chocolates and my tray and went to the front door. I rang the bell, hoping that Lindy would be on the watch for me, so I could hand her the chocolates and leave.

But no. The door was opened by a tall man of maybe forty. He had a particularly engaging grin, a turned-up nose, and long arms and legs. His blond hair had been styled by an expensive shop. He wore khakis and a navy blue knit shirt, with a matching navy blue golf sweater over it. His only jewelry was a gold ring worn on his little finger.

"Mrs. Woodyard?"

I nodded.

"Hi. I'm Rhett, the butler."

He got his laugh. I chortled out loud. It was impossible to look at his friendly, boyish face, to hear his self-effacing identification, and not feel welcomed.

"Please come in," Rhett said.

"You're not really named Rhett Butler?"

"No, but I am named Rhett. Rhett Spivey. My job title is household manager, but my duties aren't too far off from those of an old-fashioned butler. I take care of the mundane details like food and clothing, so Mr. Endicott doesn't have to. But you're the person carrying the silver salver."

"Am I? I always wondered what a salver was." I fanned myself with the plastic tray. "This one's not sterling. I brought the picnic ware today."

"Picnic is pretty close to what we're having for lunch."

I followed Rhett through a giant room circled by white pillars. It must have been an entry hall, but it seemed as big as a basketball court. Or maybe it just felt like a basketball court because of the expanse of highly polished wood flooring or because of the high ceiling. When I looked up I saw the inside of the main dome.

Through the pillars on the right I could see a living room. The room seemed to be full of men, all of them wearing expensive sports clothes. Cashmere sweaters, camel hair jackets, and loafers with that handmade look were everywhere. A few of the guys glanced at me, but I was obviously wallpaper to the confab.

I ignored them, just the way they were ignoring me, and looked left. On that side was a large, casual dining room. Neither the living room nor the dining room matched the overdone outside of the house; both were comfortable, but not pretentious.

The living room was furnished with sectionals in earth tones—matching the room in scale, but not massive—and the dining room held two large dining tables of light birch. Both rooms had gold-toned walls with lots of texture, the sort of paint job that requires twenty-five coats of glaze, each applied by a highly skilled artisan. I once had a living room with that kind of paint job. I was glad to leave it behind in Dallas.

The kitchen was visible through a door at the back of the dining room as we went in. "I'm impressed," I said. "Your kitchen looks like a display at the home show."

Rhett Spivey laughed. "Yeah, except that they shorted the parking for the help."

I peeked through the window. The Herrera van and a white Cadillac Escalade were parked there. Rhett drove an Escalade? Endicott must pay him pretty well.

Lindy, wearing a white jacket to show she was on duty, was at the back of the dining room, arranging baskets of silverware.

"Mrs. Herrera is a real godsend to me," Rhett said as we reached Lindy's end of the room. "She's even offered to help me locate some staff to fill in while we're here."

"We have to lay off bunches of employees when Warner Pier closes up for the winter," Lindy said. "So I know lots of people who can take on some short-term jobs. I could even find you a cook."

"It might be safer for Herrera's to continue providing the food," Rhett said. "I have no idea how long we'll be here. Any or all of these guys may leave on a moment's notice. So it's smarter not to stock up. If I just can find someone to help with the bed making and dishes, and you'll continue to deliver food, we'll manage."

I took a peek into the living room. "Are all these people staying here?"

"There are only six bedrooms. So five of the guests are at bed-and-breakfasts. But they're all eating here."

As he talked, Rhett opened one of the TenHuis boxes and took out a double fudge bonbon. ("Layers of milk and dark chocolate fudge with a dark chocolate coating.")

He nibbled it, then opened his eyes in a lively display of pleasure. "Wahhoo! We've got at least three people in this crowd who are going to go for these. You'd better send us two or three more boxes." He took another bite. "Or maybe four."

I laughed. "You mean it's possible to be a top exec and a chocoholic at the same time?"

"Oh, they don't deny themselves any of life's little pleasures. And luckily the staff gets to eat the same food the boss does." Rhett took my faux silver tray and began arranging the chocolates. "How'd Mr. Ludlum find out about TinHouse Chocolates?"

"My husband used to work with him," I said. "And, just for the record, our company's name rhymes with 'ice' and we use the Dutch word for chocolate. It's 'Ten Hice Chocolade.' "

"Sorry, Mrs. Woodyard!"

"No problem. That's the way I said it when I arrived from Texas. And if I'm calling you Rhett, you should call me Lee."

"No can do. I make it a policy to use titles for everyone. That way I don't forget them at the wrong time." Rhett smiled. "Mr. Ludlum's upstairs. I'll find him."

"Why?"

"He wanted to see you."

I groaned inwardly. Then I started helping Lindy fold heavy cotton napkins. But within two or three minutes I heard footsteps coming toward me and turned to face Marty Ludlum.

"Lee!" Marty tried to grab my hands. They were full of napkins, however, so he grabbed my shoulders, his face screwed into a sympathetic grimace.

"Lee! What a horrible experience you had last night!"

He was laying it on so thick that I was tickled and deliberately misinterpreted his remark. "Joe and I don't find it all that upsetting when people drop in unexpectedly, Marty."

He relaxed the grimace slightly. "Lee, I just heard about you and your aunt stumbling across a body. You're putting on a brave face, but it must have been a terrible shock."

"It wasn't a lot of fun, which is why I didn't want to talk about it last night. But it isn't as if it were someone I knew well."

"Knew well? I didn't realize that you knew the guy at all."

"He'd called at the shop. We spoke for five minutes." I added a final napkin to Lindy's stack. "Thanks for the chocolate order."

"Thanks for bringing it out personally."

"Everybody else was busy making the stuff. Anyway, I'll head back to the office now."

"I'll walk you out."

"I think I know the way."

Marty smiled and followed me, an action I interpreted as meaning he had something to say.

But we didn't get to the front door before a voice called from the living room.

"Marty! Come in here! The bitch is on CNN."

Marty's expression changed into something very close to a pout. He rolled his eyes, just slightly. He went into the living room. At the opposite end a giant television set was blaring a news channel. "Runaway business executive Patricia Youngman, still dodging reporters' questions, today was glimpsed shopping in Johannesburg, South Africa. She fled before reporters were able to question her. Youngman is being sought as a witness in the investigation of Prodigal Corporation and its controversial CEO Marson Endicott. Authorities believe Youngman is hiding out in Namibia, which has no extradition treaty with the United States."

There was a fleeting picture of an ordinary-looking woman wearing giant sunglasses. Her hair was in a pageboy and was that medium blond that career women adopt as they hit their forties. With just a fleeting glimpse of her face, she looked more like Joe's mom than like the notorious creature whose picture had been all over the news magazines when she took a powder.

Actually, on a small-town scale, Joe's mom was much like Patricia Youngman—they were efficient managers who make sure the world runs smoothly. These people are often underestimated, until, like Patricia Youngman, they do something uncharacteristic such as fleeing with company records.

My musings were overridden by the colorful swearing coming from the living room. I retreated toward the front door, but I'd seen enough to know it wasn't Marson Endicott who was swearing. I spotted him sitting motionless on one of the sectionals. His beautiful head of white hair was easy to identify; I'd seen it enough on television.

No, the swearing was coming from some hard-eyed guy with a bald head and a crooked nose. He was cutting loose at the television set at the top of his voice. I had the sense that I'd seen him before. As one of Endicott's hangers-on, he must have been on CNN or in a news magazine, probably looming in the background.

I didn't care who he was. I didn't want to witness this scene. I went outside, closed the door behind myself, and stood on the porch, wondering if I should continue waiting for Marty Ludlum or if I should simply leave.

Before I could decide, the door opened and Marty popped out. "Don't leave yet. I had a question for you."

I waited while he took several deep breaths. "Lee, are you the reason Joe doesn't want to go back into law?"

I took longer to answer than he had taken to ask. The question had surprised me. I didn't want to stumble over my answer.

"Marty, I assure you that Joe does what he wants about his legal career. I would appreciate it if he let me know before he decided to make a major job change, but he's a big boy. He decides for himself."

"Then you would have no objection to him going back into the practice of law?"

"I'd be amazed if he did. But I want Joe to be happy. If that would make him happy, fine."

"Even if you had to move."

"Warner Pier would survive without us. Aunt Nettie could

find another business manager. We'd have no trouble selling our house."

"Even though your grandfather built it?"

"If Joe were to make the kind of money you were talking about last night, we could keep it as a summer cottage."

"You'd have to leave your hometown."

"I've already left my hometown. My hometown is Prairie Creek, Texas."

I tried to keep a pleasant expression, but I was getting annoyed. "Marty, this conversation is lucrative. I mean, ludicrous! Why are you asking me? Does Joe strike you as the kind of man who would let his wife make his professional decisions? Ask Joe."

I turned toward my van. "Make *him* an offer. He and I will talk it over, and he'll tell you what *he* decides."

Marty Ludlum followed me to the van. "I didn't mean to annoy you, Lee. I'm just trying to figure out why Joe seems afraid to help me out."

"Help you out? By going to work for your firm?"

"No! No, I need help here in Warner Pier."

"Help here? Doing what?"

Marty smiled. "Local knowledge. Just background. An ear to the ground."

I almost asked him what he needed to know. I have a lot of local knowledge about Warner Pier myself. And I sure did want to know what was going on.

But I remembered Joe had given a firm "no" the previous evening when Marty asked him about local knowledge. So I restrained myself. I merely got in the van, said good-bye, and drove off. Still curious.

Why on earth was Joe declining to give an old friend "background"? What had Marty Ludlum wanted to know about Warner Pier that Joe didn't want to tell him? It obviously wasn't the population or the tax rate. It wasn't the zoning regulations. It must be something about people who lived or visited there, something that Joe didn't feel free to discuss.

And how did Joe know in advance that Marty wanted information he wouldn't feel free to hand out?

Why was Joe distancing himself from someone he had apparently once regarded as a friend? Why had he asked me not to leave him alone with Marty?

Well, at least I'd seen the fabulous Endicott house. And I'd gotten a peek at the fabulous Marson Endicott himself and at his fabulous entourage. Including the guy with the potty mouth.

The security gate opened magically before me, and I realized someone must be keeping an eye on it through the electronic monitoring system. And as I drove through I realized why Potty Mouth had seemed so familiar to me.

Bald head. Crooked nose. Tough looks.

Potty Mouth was one of the guys who had been closeted with Joe and Hogan in the police station right before Aunt Nettie and I stumbled over Derrick Valentine's body.

Chapter 8

I wasn't quite back to town when my cell phone rang. When I managed to dig it out of the bottom of my purse I saw that the caller was Joe's mom. Before Mercy got to the main reason for her call, I had to assure her that neither Aunt Nettie nor I had been traumatized by finding a dead man. But her true concern came out fairly soon.

"Mike and I are rescheduling our dinner for tomorrow night," she said. "Tony and Lindy have some school function tonight. I talked to Joe, and he says he thinks he can make it then."

"He'd better!"

"Is tomorrow all right for you?"

"Sure. Same time?"

"Yes." Mercy paused. "Joe seems absentminded today. What's eating him?"

"I don't know." She didn't say anything, so I spoke again. "I really don't, Mercy."

"Something is bothering him."

"I know. But he's not confiding in me."

"That old friend of his is in town."

"Old friend?"

Mercy sounded excited. "Yes, that big defense lawyer. Marvin Ludlum. He's representing Marson Endicott, and they've showed up here for some sort of conference on his case. I saw it on CNN."

"I know. I've just been out to the Dome Home delivering chocolate for their lunch. And Marty Ludlum dropped in on us last night. But Joe didn't talk as if they were close friends."

"In the past the old firm has used Ludlum to—well, liaise with Joe. Did he offer him a job again?"

"Not exactly."

"If it's not that situation, what else could be bothering Joe?"

"Gosh, Mercy! He could be worried about some boat. Whether it should have a red stripe or a blue one. You know Joe."

"You're right." Mercy sighed. "If he gives you a hint, please pass it on to me. And don't let him forget tomorrow."

She hung up before I could say that I'd tried to remind Joe about the important dinner the previous evening, and it hadn't done any good. Could it be that Joe was trying to avoid learning about any plans his mom and her boyfriend had made? Maybe this called for a confrontation. I decided that I'd make an effort to track Joe down and quiz him.

I pulled the van over, got out the cell phone, and rearranged my schedule. I called the office and asked Aunt Nettie if she'd heard from anybody, such as Myrl or Sarajane. She hadn't. I told her I wouldn't be back until around two o'clock. I called Lindy and told her I couldn't meet her until one o'clock.

Then I called Sarajane; I hadn't forgotten the two o'clock deadline I'd given her, and it was then after twelve. She answered the phone so quickly that I felt sure she was still waiting for a call from Myrl. And she sounded so disappointed to hear my voice—I wasn't Myrl—that I felt sorry for her. I guess that was why I gave her another hour. Besides, she promised renewed efforts to call all the underground railroad people she could think of during that hour, checking to see if any of them had heard from Myrl or Pamela.

Then I headed for Vintage Boats, where Joe hangs out most of his working days.

Joe's boat shop is on the inland edge of Warner Pier, on the Warner River, upstream from the main part of the town. He doesn't know how much longer he'll be able to hang on to the ten-acre site. Waterfront property, either lake or river, is valuable in Warner Pier, so his taxes keep going up. Some day a Marson Endicott look-alike is going to show up and offer him too much money to justify keeping the property to use for a forty-year-old metal building he could rebuild on any lot. Then he'll have to move the shop some place inland and give up having a private dock on a river that has access to Lake Michigan. He'll hate losing his dock, but he should make enough money to rebuild for cash and pay off his current mortgage. When he gets the right offer.

I pulled into the driveway and realized I wasn't Joe's only visitor. A Warner Pier police cruiser was parked beside Joe's truck. I recognized the number on the cruiser; Hogan was there.

I didn't know why Joe and Hogan had suddenly become best buddies, but I suspected that I wasn't going to get a word out of either of them while they could link their mental shields together into a wall of none-of-your-business.

However, this was the perfect time to talk to Hogan privately about Sarajane, Myrl, Pamela, and the dadgum underground railroad. I considered this. But not ten minutes earlier I'd promised Sarajane that I'd wait.

I decided I couldn't talk to Hogan yet. I told myself that I'd get Sarajane to go with me to see Hogan in a couple of hours. I'd given up on hearing from Myrl and Pamela.

But the purpose of this visit was to find out what Joe was up to, and Hogan's presence might keep me from applying the third degree. Was it worth going in? I decided that I could at least back up Mercy's dinner invitation. I parked the van and went into the shop.

I didn't see either Joe or Hogan right away. Then the door to the one-room apartment at the back of the shop opened about a foot, and Joe looked out. He didn't look happy to see me.

"We're back here," he said. "Eating lunch."

I stamped the snow off my feet—Joe clears only a small area of his gravel parking lot—and walked back to the inner chamber. Joe lived in that room for four years after he bought the business, sleeping on a twin bed and cooking on a hot plate. He had given his twin bed away, but the room still has an old recliner, a hot plate, a small refrigerator, and a kitchen table and chairs. A dinky bathroom with a shower adjoins.

He and Hogan were eating grilled cheese sandwiches. Hogan, who couldn't have had more than two or three hours of sleep, looked more like Abraham Lincoln than usual. In fact, he looked like Abraham Lincoln at a time the great man must have been extremely worried about the progress of the Civil War.

"I'll bet Joe will make one of his extra-special grilled cheese sandwiches for you, too, Lee," he said.

"I'm meeting Lindy for lunch at one," I said. "I just dropped by to double-check with Joe about our second try at dinner with Mercy and Mike. Now it's set for tomorrow night."

Joe sighed. "I know. I promise I'll make it this time."

I pulled up a chair. "Incidentally, I just ran into that guy you two had cornered yesterday."

"What guy we had cornered?" Hogan sounded surprised.

"The bald guy who was in your office yesterday."

Hogan laughed. "We didn't have him cornered."

Joe looked at me sharply. "You didn't say anything to him?"

"No, darling." I let the slightest tone of sarcasm creep into my voice. "You said not to. Besides, it wasn't a face-to-face meeting. He was in Marson Endicott's living room, swearing up a storm, and I was in the front hall."

They spoke at the same time. "What were you doing in Marson Endicott's front hall?"

I explained about the chocolate, but I left my brief conversation with Marty Ludlum out of the report. I'd tell Joe about that privately.

"Anyway, as I left I saw that bald guy," I said. "He was concentrating on the television set. Patricia Youngman was on CNN, and he was cursing her until I was surprised that the TV set didn't slap his face."

Neither of them offered more information. They just exchanged meaningful glances and chewed.

I turned to Hogan. "Anything new on Derrick Valentine?"

"Not that I know about. Thanks to Nettie, I've been tossed out of a local investigation—and out of my own office."

"Yeah. When the police chief's wife falls over a body, it makes it look as if you might not be able to be a nonprejudiced investigator. Have they questioned Valentine's partner?"

"They're not telling me." Hogan grinned. "Joe says you sent him on the run."

"My previous experiences with private eyes were not good. I wasn't pleased to meet him. Or Valentine, for that matter." Both Hogan and Joe knew that when I left my ex-husband, Rich Godfrey, in Dallas, he decided that I wouldn't be dumping one wealthy man unless I already had another one on the string. He hired detectives to prove it. For a couple of weeks I couldn't go anywhere without seeing a nondescript vehicle in my rearview mirror. I wasn't dating anyone else—rich or poor—so all the detectives did was waste Rich's money. But the whole experience was distasteful, to say the least. It would have been terrifying if the wife of one of Rich's friends hadn't given me a broad hint about why strange men were following me.

"I don't suppose you're willing to tell me who sent Valentine and O'Sullivan to Warner Pier," I said.

"Nope." Hogan's voice was firm.

I was being stonewalled. I hate when that happens. So I got a bit outrageous.

"I guess the mob wouldn't hire private eyes," I said.

Joe rolled his eyes and laughed. Hogan gulped hard and nearly choked on his sandwich.

"Mob!" he said. "Where'd you get an idea the mob is involved?"

"Internet," I said. "Valentine was looking for a woman named Christina Meachum. I Googled her."

"And you discovered . . . ?"

"Christina Meachum was the maiden name of Christina Belcher. As in wife of Belcher the Butcher. Detroit mob."

Hogan snorted. "To the Detroit mob Christina Belcher is small potatoes."

"You don't think she's a mob target?"

"No. The people she implicated were low level. Disposable. I admit the mob might be after some of *those* guys. I'm sure the FBI flipped some of them—got them to turn state's evidence. But Christina knew very little about her husband's operation. The feds only used Christina as a crowbar to try to open a minor door to the mob."

"But if Christina Belcher isn't a mob target, why was she in the Federal Witness Protection Program?"

"I didn't know that she was."

I thought about that. "The newspaper articles I saw—"

Hogan cut in. "I never heard of the feds telling the news media that they were putting someone into the Federal Witness Protection Program. If that was in a newspaper, it was simply a guess. And it might be wrong. It also might be right. But Christina may have disappeared on her own. There's no way of telling."

Hogan suddenly threw his head up like a deer who had sniffed a hunter with a great big rifle. He looked at me sharply. "Lee, you haven't mentioned this mob idea around town, I hope."

"I just got around to Googling Christina this morning. No, I hadn't mentioned it to anyone."

"Don't! I have enough trouble dealing with rumors in Warner Pier without the populace deciding we're being invaded by the Detroit mob."

Joe and I both laughed, and I promised I wouldn't mention the possibility of mob involvement in Warner Pier's crime scene. Then I left to meet Lindy for lunch. But before I went out the door I casually asked Hogan where he planned to be that afternoon. I didn't tell Hogan why I wanted to know, but I was hoping Sarajane and I would need to talk to him in a couple of hours.

I drove toward the Sidewalk Café. I was looking forward to a visit with Lindy, even if I had to guard my tongue, because she always cheers me up. So it was disheartening when—as soon as we'd slid into a booth and ordered sandwiches—she opened the conversation by saying, "Lee, I'm almost at the end of my rope."

I tried to keep the party light. "You must feel like my Texas grandma used to. She'd say, 'I'm ready to cut my suspenders and go straight up.' "

The down-home witticism fell flat. Lindy blinked hard, and I realized she was trying not to cry. She spoke, and her voice sounded frantic. "I can't cry here! Not in front of Herrera employees, not when Mike might walk in any moment!"

"Lean over and pop your contacts out," I said. "That'll give you an excuse for watery eyes. Here's a Kleenex. And when you get the contacts out, I'll be ready to listen."

"Thanks." Her voice croaked.

"You've listened to my problems often enough." I waited until she got the contacts out and mopped her eyes.

When she spoke again, her voice was close to normal. "It's Tony."

"What's he done?"

"All of a sudden he's all upset because I make more money than he does."

"Lots of guys would think that was a good thing. But neither of you has changed jobs lately. Why is that bothering Tony now?"

The waiter brought our drinks, and Lindy stared at her napkin until he had left. "He just figured it out."

"Tony didn't know how much money you made?"

"Lee, he doesn't even know how much he makes himself!

I've always handled the family finances." Lindy fought back tears again. "You know that Tony always refused to work in one of Mike's restaurants."

"Really? The first summer I worked here—when we were sixteen—I thought Tony was working at Herrera's."

"Mike tried to get him to work there. He started him as a busboy. Tony was so rude to the customers that Mike had to fire him. Frankly, Tony has always thought waiting on people—even serving them good food that they pay a lot for—is menial."

"Tony's like Joe. They're happier working with their hands."

"Tony is. I've always wanted him to do something he liked doing. So the machine shop was fine with me."

"Did he mind you working at what he thinks is a menial job?" Lindy started as a waitress, and she'd also worked as a cook.

Lindy laughed ruefully. "I'm only a woman, Lee. Tony has a strong streak of machismo, you know. A menial job was good enough for a woman."

"But you quit waiting tables five years ago. Now that you're catering manager . . ." I got it. "Oh. You didn't tell Tony that you're making good money now that you're in charge of one of Mike's main business enterprises."

Lindy shook her head. "I guess I should have gone into the details more. I think Tony had the idea that Mike was paying me as a way to help out his grandchildren. When he realized that I have—well, major responsibilities, that I hire and fire, that I bid on major banquets and weddings and that the business is quite successful . . ."

"I wouldn't want to guess at the annual business Herrera Catering does, but you're in charge of all of it."

"Yes. But Tony had never realized what my responsibilities and my salary were until this situation with Mercy and Mike came up. I mean, the obvious thing is that they're planning to get married, and it made Tony think about his dad's property."

"With three restaurants and the catering company . . . Does Mike own his own buildings?"

"He owns this one and the building where Herrera's is. He leases the other restaurant. But see, Tony had always seen Mike's business as just small-town restaurants. This was the first time that he looked at what a successful businessman his dad is."

"And now he's kicking himself for not sticking it out as a busboy."

Tears welled up in Lindy's eyes again. "Oh, Lee, Tony would be terrible in the restaurant business!"

"Yes, he would. He'd hate every minute of it, and you'd be his boss."

"I knew you'd see the problem!"

Lindy dabbed at her eyes again, and I thought before I spoke. "Does Tony feel as if he should start taking an interest?"

"Yes. He sees that he's Mike's main heir. Of course, that may change if Mike and Mercy get married."

"Mercy has a successful business of her own. Joe and I are certainly not interested in inheriting from Mike."

"I know—I mean, I thought you'd feel that way. But suddenly Tony feels as if he's failed his dad by never taking any interest in the business. Now he thinks maybe he should try."

"And he'd rather be shot."

Lindy finally smiled. "Basically. Plus, he sees that I've been down there learning the ropes for ten years."

"You'd have to break him in." I thought a moment, then went on. "Tony's smart enough to learn anything he sets his mind on, of course, but I think he'd be making a mistake if he tried the restaurant business at this point."

"Yes, he doesn't meet the public easily, and he isn't interested in the business side." Lindy's voice rose. "He doesn't even like to cook!"

I thought about Lindy's problem and stirred my iced tea. Us Texans, we like iced tea all year round, and Mike's restaurants are the only places in Warner Pier where I can get it in the winter. And it's good tea, too. That's because Mike came to Michigan from Denton, Texas, more than forty years ago. He understands iced tea. I took a big drink from my glass before I went on.

"Listen, Lindy, I can't believe Mike hasn't thought this through. He and Tony get along pretty well these days, don't they?"

"Once Mike gave up trying to force Tony into the restaurant business, things have been fine between them. To be honest, I think Mike would be horrified if Tony tried to come back."

She leaned across the table and spoke earnestly. "Do you think Joe could talk to Tony?"

"I don't know if that would help, but I'll ask him."

Our sandwiches came, and we left it at that. For the rest of the lunch I caught up on Lindy's parents and her kids and stayed away from discussing her job.

We were still in the restaurant when my cell phone rang. The caller ID said it was the chocolate shop. I answered. "Yes."

"Lee, Lee!" It was Aunt Nettie, and she was excited. It scared me.

"What's wrong, Aunt Nettie?"

"Nothing's wrong, Lee. Everything's all right. Sarajane got a phone call from Pamela."

Chocolate Chat
Chocolate Forms

Chocolate for eating comes in three basic flavors: Dark, milk, and—maybe—white.

Dark chocolate is sweetened chocolate liquor that contains no milk solids. These days dark chocolate packaging lists the percentage of cocoa in the product. This refers to the total amount of ingredients derived from cacao. Higher percentages, however, may not guarantee a higher-quality product.

Milk chocolate was invented in the mid-nineteenth century when Henri Nestlé, who had discovered how to make powdered milk, got together with chocolatier Daniel Peter. They figured out how to replace the moisture in cocoa with cacao butter and add milk, so it could be molded. Result: the first milk chocolate bar.

White chocolate, purists believe, isn't chocolate at all, since it is made with cocoa butter only. In the United States it is called "white confectionery coating."

Chapter 9

"Where are they?"

"Pamela didn't tell Sarajane that. But she says she and Myrl are safe."

My excitement cooled to a simmer. A phone call from Pamela was good, true. But I needed more details before I would be happy.

"I'll run by Sarajane's and get a firsthand account," I said.

Of course, I had another purpose for talking to Sarajane, one I didn't mention to Aunt Nettie. If Pamela was away safely, it was time for me to tell Hogan and the State Police that she was the woman Derrick Valentine had been looking for. But I felt that I had to warn Sarajane before I did that.

I said good-bye to Lindy, promising to talk to Joe about her problem with Tony. I paid my bill, jumped into the van, and pointed it toward Sarajane's combined home and business, the Peach Street Bed-and-Breakfast Inn.

The one-hundred-twenty-five-year-old Queen Anne Victorian that houses the B&B is located on the outskirts of Warner Pier. As I pulled up I saw that a stuffed fabric snowman left over from a recent tourism promotion still decorated its broad porch. Not that the sprawling structure needed any extra trim. Every eave was already dripping with gingerbread. The sun had come out, and the afternoon had grown warm enough to encourage a few icicles, so the house glittered as if it were trimmed with rhinestone fringe.

I went to the back door, since Sarajane uses that door for everything personal. She had apparently heard me drive up; the door opened as I came up the steps. Behind Sarajane I saw that a chest of drawers that stood in the back hall had been moved away from the wall. Several of the drawers were pulled out.

"Are you moving furniture?" I said.

"No. I was just looking for something I misplaced. Come in."

"I was so glad to hear that Pamela had called," I said.

"I was terribly relieved to hear from her," Sarajane said. "Of course, I knew Myrl can handle anything. But when they didn't arrive . . . it was scary."

"Aunt Nettie said Pamela didn't tell you where they were."

"No, she just said they were well away from Warner Pier."

I realized that while Sarajane might be claiming she was relieved, she still looked worried.

Sarajane always wears rather masculine clothes—jeans, tailored pants suits, slacks, and sweaters—but she has one of those extremely feminine faces, with dimples and round cheeks. Now her dimples were barely visible, and her eyebrows were sloping toward her ears, giving her a woebegone look.

"What's wrong?" I said.

"Nothing! Nothing is wrong." Sarajane motioned toward the chest of drawers. "I was just looking for something."

I wasn't concerned about that. "Did you get the phone number Pamela called from?"

Sarajane shook her head. "I don't have caller ID. But Pamela said she was using Myrl's cell phone, so the number wouldn't have helped locate them. They could be calling from anywhere."

"Yes, if they started driving at four a.m. they've had ten hours to go elsewhere. They could be—way beyond Indianapolis by now. Or past Chicago and nearly into Missouri."

"They could be in Canada." Sarajane's voice was quiet.

"Canada! I wouldn't think Myrl would take Pamela out of the country. Even if she had a passport . . ."

"She did."

"Pamela had a passport?" I was astonished. I knew that the underground railroad had to use faked driver's licenses and other identification papers, though I didn't think Pamela had any of those. If she had a Social Security number, even a false one, why did I have to pay her off the books?

But the idea of a faked passport shocked me. Having a fake passport would be a serious offense. Surely Pamela hadn't had one. "How do you know Pamela had a passport?"

"I saw it once. I took clean sheets up to her room while she was at work. She'd left that duffel bag on the bed. I accidentally knocked it off, and the passport fell out of the side pocket."

"Was it in her real name? Or her—nom de guerre?"

"I didn't open it. I guess it could have been somebody else's passport."

"That doesn't seem likely."

"No, it doesn't."

"It seems funny that Pamela called you. Instead of Myrl making the call."

"She said Myrl had gone out to get them something to eat." Sarajane's eyebrows were still slanting at that worried angle.

"Sarajane," I said. "What's bothering you?"

"Bothering me?"

"Yes, you don't seem happy."

She smiled tightly. "Lee, I've just spent the morning worrying so hard that I can't seem to stop. But everything is all right."

"Are you sure?"

"What could be wrong? Myrl got Pamela away safely. That was my main concern."

"Okay," I said. "Now to the next problem. Derrick Valentine."

Sarajane sniffed. "I don't consider him my problem."

"But he was killed, Sarajane. Beaten to death. We can't just ignore it."

"I can."

"But we don't know who killed him! It might be someone still roaming around town. Someone else might be in danger."

"I don't think so, Lee. I think he was mugged. That Valentine fellow was just walking around looking for trouble."

"In Warner Pier? There's rarely any of that kind of trouble here. Plus, why would he look for trouble in our alley?"

"I don't know! But I do know that Myrl does not want any attention from the police."

"But Valentine was looking for Pamela! And she was actually here. That's a valuable clue."

"Pamela had nothing to do with Valentine's death. She was here with me all evening."

"I don't think she actually struck the blow that killed him, Sarajane. But she has some connection with him or he wouldn't have been looking for her."

"I don't see how that can be true. I don't think she knew anything about Derrick Valentine."

"Ye gods, Sarajane! We've got to tell the detectives about this. If we don't we might all be charged as accessories to Valentine's murder."

"Accessories? That's silly."

"Well, we could be accused of obstructing justice, then. It's not . . ." Words almost failed me, but I plowed on. "It's not lawful, Sarajane."

The response I got to that remark was nonverbal, but it said more than a thousand words could have. Sarajane simply looked at me. Her face showed almost no expression. She didn't say a word, but she might as well have yelled her reply out. And that reply was, "So what?"

I stared at her. She stared at me. I was the one who blinked.

"I know, I know," I said. "You think the law has failed these women. That people like you and Myrl are justified in doing just about anything to help them."

Sarajane nodded.

"But the law will continue to fail all of us," I said, "if citizens don't respect it, if they don't support law enforcement."

I got the stony stare again. But she did speak. "I'm sorry, Lee. I can't do anything to endanger this system of protecting women. It's too valuable. It's needed in so many cases."

She reached over and touched my arm. "Lee, I'm sorry we had to ask for your help. But you're not part of this. You have to follow your own conscience. If you feel compelled to talk to the police—even though it might wreck our system—then you must do it."

I felt so frustrated that I wanted to slam my fist into something. Maybe Sarajane's nose. But I resisted. How could Sarajane *always* put me in the wrong? She knew I couldn't tell the police about her underground railroad operation if she thought it would endanger abused women.

Frustrated, I turned toward the door.

"If I decide to talk to the police, I'll let you know." I gestured toward the chest of drawers she'd been ransacking. "Do you need help with this chest?"

"No! No, I've simply misplaced something. I thought it might have fallen behind the chest, but it's not there. I can move the chest back by myself."

I didn't press her. I just went out the back door and climbed into the van. I was furious. But I didn't want to go against Sarajane's opinion.

I had resisted bopping Sarajane on the nose, but I did slam my fist onto the steering wheel a few times as I drove along. And I spoke aloud to express my frustration.

"Golly! Gee whiz! Dadgum!" I said. Or something like that.

As I drew near the office I realized that I wasn't just angry with Sarajane. Some memory was trying to jump out of my subconscious. It wasn't anything about the argument Sarajane and I had had. It was something about that chest she'd been searching. I was clear back to the shop before I realized what it was.

I recalled an earlier visit to the Peach Street B&B. I'd come in that same back door, and the top drawer in that chest had been slightly ajar. As I had walked by it, I had seen what was in the drawer.

A pistol.

I didn't gasp or throw my hands up when I remembered

the pistol. Actually, I felt relief at identifying my memory, and I shrugged the whole thing off.

I shrugged it off because Sarajane had once told me that because of the lonely situation of the B&B she slept with a pistol in her bedside table. I interpreted this to mean that she didn't usually store it in that chest in the kitchen. At the time I'd seen it, she'd been in a period of stress over a previous underground railroad passenger.

So she wouldn't have been looking for the pistol in the chest of drawers, I told myself. It was some other lost object. And whatever it was, it was none of my business. TenHuis Chocolade, on the other hand, was my business—job-wise. I headed for the office.

Once there, however, I found I could hardly work. I opened my computer, then stared blankly at the screen, trying to deal with my feelings of frustration. I tried to accept the situation. Sarajane had me over the traditional barrel—I could not go to the police and tell them the woman Derrick Valentine had been looking for had been there all the time. And I recognized another part to the problem. I wasn't terribly interested in telling the proper authorities Derrick Valentine had come to Warner Pier looking for Christina-Pamela. Not doing my legal duty didn't disturb me a whole heck of a lot.

No, the main thing I wanted was to find out the answers to three questions: How? Who? Why?

How had Derrick Valentine known Christina was in Warner Pier?

Who had hired him?

Why?

Answering the first question might explain the second

question, of course, and answering the first two could answer the third.

The logical person who might be looking for Christina-Pamela was her husband, Harold Belcher. Christina-Pamela believed he wanted to kill her. And he couldn't kill her until he could find her.

But why would he hire private detectives to find her? If they located her and told Belcher the Butcher where she was and she subsequently turned up dead—well, the culprit would be pretty obvious. I would think even a sleazy private eye might see a connection. And unless that private eye was dumber than dirt, he'd see that he had put himself in Belcher's power, and he'd go to the cops. Or else he'd threaten Belcher with what he knew.

Neither scenario made it likely that Harold Belcher would have hired a private eye to find his ex-wife.

But what did seem likely? I'd asked both Derrick Valentine and Tom O'Sullivan why they had thought Christina was at TenHuis Chocolade.

Valentine's answer had been gruff. "Information received." But O'Sullivan had almost goofed. He'd started to say something that began with "f." "Fink?" "Fury?"

I looked around my desk. How about "phone"?

Hmmm.

Christina could have used the TenHuis Chocolade phone, of course. She could have called someone. If that person had caller ID, they'd know the number. She might even have given someone the number and asked that person to call her back.

TenHuis Chocolade has two phone lines, and either can be used in three places. My office, the cash register, and the break room all have extensions. Christina-Pamela had never used the phone in the office, at least while I was there, and I'd never seen her near the phone behind the cash register. But she could easily have used the extension in the break room.

I went into the workroom, where Aunt Nettie was standing over a wonderful copper kettle, part of a chocolatier's traditional equipment. She used it to make the fillings for her luscious chocolates. The kettle is about two and a half feet in diameter and is eight or ten inches deep. It sits enthroned on a metal stand that also holds its own gas burner. Aunt Nettie had loaded the kettle with cream, butter, and sugar. She was stirring the potion, and—I believe—muttering incantations. At least it seemed to me that the fabulous concoctions she made in that kettle could only have been produced by magic.

I asked her if she'd ever seen Pamela using the telephone. "No," she said.

Which didn't mean Pamela hadn't done it when neither of us was around. Of course, I could check on the long distance calls. But I had no way of knowing about local calls. I wasn't even sure the phone company would be willing to give me that information, though Hogan had told me law enforcement agencies can get it.

Forget it, I told myself.

I tried to think about work. I checked my e-mail, printing out two new orders for Easter bunnies, but I couldn't concentrate on the job. Since I was online and still curious, I Googled Harold Belcher. What I found distracted me even further.

According to a story in the previous day's *Detroit Free Press*, Harold Belcher was out of prison.

Belcher had completed his sentence for his chop shop activities. He was appealing his conviction in the wife-beating case. The judge had ruled he should be released until his appeal was denied or upheld.

"Rats!" I said.

I could only hope that neither PDQ Investigations nor anyone else had told Harold where Christina had been hanging out. I did not want a guy with the nickname "the Butcher" dropping by to see if she was working at TenHuis Chocolade.

But what could I do about it? I pulled out the photo of Belcher I'd printed out earlier and looked at it.

I needed advice. I called Hogan.

I didn't tell him that Christina-Pamela had been working at TenHuis Chocolade and had been spirited away in the middle of the previous night. I told him that Derrick Valentine and Tom O'Sullivan had come to TenHuis Chocolade because they thought she had been there. I told him I was afraid they might have told Harold that.

"Because who else could be their client?" I said.

Hogan made soothing sounds, but he didn't deny that I had a valid concern.

I went on. "So what do we do if he shows up?"

"I wouldn't expect him to come busting in the door firing a tommy gun," Hogan said. "One of the scariest things I've heard about Belcher—and I haven't had any connection with the case, of course—is that he's quite cold-blooded. If he offed someone in the course of his job with the mob, he did it so coolly that the FBI hasn't been able to prove anything. Apparently the only person he ever hit in anger was his wife."

"I don't find that reassuring."

Hogan sighed. "I don't either. I'll pass your concern on to the State Police. Frankly, at the moment Warner Pier is full of state cops because of the killing of Valentine, so I'd expect

Belcher to avoid the place. If he has any interest in coming here. And we don't know that he does have any such interest."

He repeated his promise to alert his officers and the state cops who were around town, telling them that Belcher had been released.

As soon as I hung up the phone, I locked the front door. It just made me feel better. We don't have much walk-in traffic in the winter. I left the OPEN sign up. If a customer knocked, I'd go let him in.

Unless the customer was a big, bald guy with a crooked nose.

Then I called Joe and told him I'd have to stay late at work that night. I had completely wasted the whole afternoon.

"Will you have time to get a pizza at the Dock Street for the second night in a row?" Joe said. The Dock Street Pizza Place is Warner Pier's handiest place for a quick dinner.

"I guess so," I said. "Or you could pick one up and bring it by here."

"It'll do you good to get away for a few minutes. I'll go by there, get a booth, and order. Then I'll call you. You can take half an hour away from the office."

I agreed. Which is why we found ourselves in a booth at the Dock Street when Gregory Glossop walked up to the table.

Greg Gossip—I mean, Glossop—is one of my least favorite people. He operates the pharmacy at the Superette, the one place in Warner Pier where groceries are sold. He sits up in a high office overlooking the store, he sees everyone who comes in, and he checks out which aisles they visit. If an older couple buys baby food, he knows their grandchildren are coming.

When customers get prescriptions filled, he pumps them. I can't point to any occasion on which he's passed on information about his customer's health issues—I'm sure Greg would find *that* unprofessional—but he sure passes on everything else he hears. And he hears a lot.

So I wasn't thrilled when Greg came by to table-hop. He was sure either to tell us something or to ask us something we didn't want to know.

Sure enough, after a few preliminaries, Greg turned to Joe. "Is there some city problem out at the Lake Michigan Inn?"

"Not that I know of."

"I'm glad to hear it." Greg's voice was jovial. "I wondered why you'd been out there."

Chapter 10

I was surprised. Greg had put an innuendo in this question that was truly ugly. Even for Greg Gossip it had been a dirty crack.

I knew it wouldn't bother Joe. Between his naturally quick wits and his legal experience, he always knows the right thing to say. I waited to hear him say, "I went out there to see a man about a boat, Greg. What's it to ya?" or something equally brilliant.

But Joe didn't say anything.

I looked at him. And darned if he hadn't grown three shades redder than usual. He looked embarrassed.

I was so astonished that I cracked up. Broke out laughing big-time.

This had the effect of making Greg look at me, which was a good thing, I guess, because it gave Joe a moment to calm his blush.

First Joe spoke to me. "What's with you?"

Then he turned to Greg. "I parked in the Lake Michigan Inn's lot while I ran over to the Stop and Shop and got a Coke from the machine outside."

I was still whooping with laughter.

Joe spoke again. "Why did you want to know, Greg?"

His question managed to abash Greg Glossop, which is no easy task. The guy buys gall by the gallon. He muttered something about concerns over zoning policies, then left the restaurant.

By the time he was out the door, I'd stopped whooping, but I still had a serious case of the giggles.

Joe looked at me with half a frown. "I'm not sure I like this."

"What?"

"When the town's biggest gossip lays out a remark that could be interpreted as a slur on my faithfulness, my wife thinks it's funny."

"It was your reaction that was funny. You were embarrassed."

"So? A couple of months back a low-down motel desk clerk got the idea you were a call girl. Did you find that amusing?"

"It made me darn mad."

"Oh? Then why should Greg's innuendo about me make you laugh?"

I was afraid I had hurt Joe's feelings. He doesn't display them much, so it's hard to tell when they've been bruised. I put down my pizza and tried to make amends.

"First, I've read that incongruity—surprise—is one of the main components of humor."

"Right. We all laugh when the guy in the top hat slips on a banana peel."

"Greg's remark caught me completely by surprise. Second, you are so quick mentally that I expected you to puncture Greg with your rapier-sharp wit. The way you finally did."

"You couldn't put off laughing until I thought of something to say?"

"Joe! You were blushing!"

"That was funny?"

"It was unexpected."

Joe took a drink of his beer. "You're not taking me for granted just because we're married, are you?"

He looked at me slyly, and I saw that he was teasing. I moved my plate, pizza and all, across the table. "Move over," I said. I got out of my side of the booth and sat down on his side, turning to face him.

"Third, bozo," I said, "the Lake Michigan Inn isn't the hot-sheets joint of choice for Warner Pier. People from Holland or Kalamazoo might check in there, but locals? Never. It's no place to do anything sneaky because Greg Glossop probably checks the parking lot on his way to and from work every day. Warner Pier people go to Grand Rapids or Kalamazoo to fool around."

"Good point."

"And the fourth reason is my ego."

"You've got a nice supply of that."

"That's right, dear heart. If you're already sleeping with the most desirable woman on the shores of Lake Michigan, why would you need to check into a motel without her?"

I gave him my most provocative look.

Joe began to laugh.

I let him finish and accepted a surreptitious hug—Joe's wary of public displays of affection—before I asked the question I wanted the answer to.

"So? What *were* you doing at the Lake Michigan Inn?"

"You heard me. I parked there while I ran over to the Stop and Shop to get a soft drink out of the machine."

Joe's face looked as bland as a piece of toast before it was loaded with butter and peach preserves. Obviously, there was more to the story. Just as obviously, he wasn't going to tell me what it was.

I tried to hide my curiosity. "More mystery, huh? Fair enough. I already ran into a couple of mysterious things today. One more won't kill me."

As we ate our pizza, I told him about my encounter with Marty Ludlum and his accusation that I was keeping Joe tied to small-time life, and about Marty's quest for background information about Warner Pier.

I ended my account with a question. "How did Marty get the idea that I can exert undue influence over your career?"

"Remember that when he knew me, Lee, I was married to Clemmie. She did influence my career. Quite a bit."

"I hope I don't do that, Joe."

"I want you to care about my work! And I care about your opinion. But you don't boss me around drastically. Besides, I'm older and wiser now than I was when I was married to Clemmie. I rebelled against her, in the end, remember."

"Then let's get one thing straight. If you want to go back to practicing law full-time, it's okay with me."

"If I decide I want to do that, I'll mention it."

"And the next question is, what is this 'local knowledge' that Marty Ludlum is after that you don't want to tell him?"

"I'm not sure what Marty is after. I just don't think it's a good time for me to get together with him. Marson Endicott and his problems ought to be the only thing Marty is thinking about right now, and I don't see how that case has any direct connection with me or with Warner Pier. I'm not interested in it."

He took a drink of his beer. "But you said you ran into two mysterious things today. Was that the second one?"

"No, the second one was Lindy. There's no real mystery about it. The mystery is how to handle it." I quickly outlined Lindy's anxiety about Tony, ending by saying, "I think Tony would be a disaster in the restaurant business."

"Yeah, and he definitely wouldn't like working for his wife or his dad." Joe gave a short, barking laugh. It wasn't a happy sound. "Tony and Lindy's problem is a lot harder to solve than Marty's."

"Maybe both of us should stay out of it."

"Probably."

"Anyway, I told Lindy I'd tell you about it."

"Yeah, and I can tell Tony . . . What? I don't see how I can say anything unless he brings it up."

I nodded and took another bite. Lindy was up a stump, and her plea for help had put Joe up there, too.

"I'm just not tactful enough to handle that one," Joe said. "I doubt anyone is."

The restaurant's door opened, and I looked up. "Maybe that guy is," I said. "He's tact personified."

Rhett the Butler had just walked in.

I waved, and he came over to the booth, his engaging grin flashing like a neon sign. I introduced him to Joe.

"I see we're all hitting the hot spot of Warner Pier tonight," Rhett said.

I laughed. "Even in the summer Warner Pier is pretty short on hot spots. Are you giving the crew at the Dome Home pizza tonight?"

"I have the evening off. I set them up for dinner in a private room at Warner Pier's other hot spot."

"The Sidewalk Café only serves lunch this time of the year, so you must mean Herrera's."

"Yes. I understand there's also a good restaurant at the Warner Point Center, but it's closed up."

"Yep. They shut down in February and March. Those are our two slowest months." I gestured at the other side of the booth. "Please join us, Rhett."

"Thanks, but I'm indulging in a luxury I don't often get. I called in an order to take back and eat in lonely splendor. I'd better check on it."

Rhett went to the counter, spoke to the waitress, and pulled out a credit card. I raised my eyebrows at Joe. "Sorry. I know you don't want to know anything about Endicott and his bunch, but . . ."

"You can't be rude to a customer. And I can see this is an interesting guy."

"He seems to know how to hit just the right balance between servility and sass."

Rhett was back. He sat down opposite us. "He says it will be five minutes. Mr. Woodyard, Mrs. Herrera tells me you're Warner Pier city attorney."

"One day a week. Mainly I restore antique powerboats. How'd you get into the butler business?"

"I was assistant manager of a hotel, and I have experience with food service. I heard about the job through the grapevine and applied."

"I guess you knew the mysterious Patricia Youngman."

"She hired me." Rhett shrugged. "So, is Warner Pier so law-abiding that they only need a lawyer one day a week?"

"The city attorney doesn't have anything to do with law enforcement. My job is to make sure the city council doesn't do anything unconstitutional. Besides, the local belief is that the tourists and summer people bring all the crime with them."

"Like that guy who was killed last night?"

"He actually *was* an out-of-towner. But, as I say, I have nothing to do with crime—commission or investigation."

"Then you can't give me the inside information on his murder?"

"I don't even know if the State Police think it *was* murder. It could have been manslaughter. Or self-defense."

Rhett focused his attention on me. "I was surprised to hear you tell Mr. Ludlum you knew the victim."

"We met for five minutes. Finding him wasn't fun."

He raised his eyebrows and leaned over the table. "You're the one I should be asking for the inside scoop."

"I haven't got it."

"You didn't see any sinister strangers running down the alley? Any suspicious sports cars speeding away?"

"I didn't see a thing except my aunt standing over him too scared to fit her key into the back door lock. Let's talk about something happier." I pasted on a smile. "How many boxes of chocolates do you want to order for tomorrow?"

Rhett raised his hands as if he were surrendering, spreading his fingers far apart. He'd taken his pinkie ring off. He looked at Joe. "She's always counting, isn't she?"

Joe had a mouth full of pizza, so he merely nodded. I answered. "I'm a number person. Sales figures, phone numbers, birthdays, license plates—I remember them. Some people have perfect pitch. I do numbers."

Rhett laughed. "I'll tell Mrs. Herrera how many chocolates we need," Rhett said. "And we will want more. The TenHuis Chocolades—am I saying it right?—went over really big."

At that moment, something else big arrived. The waitress brought over a stack of boxes. There were two cardboard boxes I knew held eight-inch pizzas, plus two plastic boxes containing salads. Balanced one on top of another, they made a small tower.

Rhett jumped up. "Whoops! Better get on my way. Nice seeing you." He was out the door like a whirlwind.

I waved good-bye. Then I turned to Joe. "Nice to know that Rhett has made a friend after only one day in Warner Pier."

"A friend? He said he was having dinner in 'lonely splendor.' "

"Yes, but he ordered two eight-inch pizzas and two salads."

"Maybe he's just hungry."

We laughed and left it at that. I was a bit annoyed with Rhett. I had praised his tact to Joe, but the questions he had asked me—about the death of Derrick Valentine—had not been tactful. They'd been the kind of questions I'd expect from Greg Glossop. They'd left a bad taste in my mouth that my pizza wasn't covering up.

Joe and I were putting our coats on when the restaurant's door opened again, and a hulking figure came in. Of course, in February in Michigan everybody is wearing such heavy coats, hats, and scarves that most people appear hulking. But this guy was unusually tall, and he was wearing a gray down jacket with eye-catching yellow stripes.

Maybe I was unusually sensitive to hulking figures because of the big, ugly guy I'd seen talking to Joe and Hogan, then had run across again out at the Dome Home. The guy who hated Patricia Youngman so much that he cursed at the television set.

Potty Mouth had a big nose, as well as a shaved head. So I looked at the newcomer closely. The big guy coming in the door also had a big schnoz. My nerves jumped when I saw it. Then he pulled his hat off, and I realized it wasn't the same man. This one had hair. Not a lot of hair, but more than Potty Mouth could have sprouted since noon that day. I breathed a sigh of relief.

I put on my own hat and zipped up my jacket, and Joe and I left. We said a warm good-bye in the parking lot, and I promised not to be at the office too long.

Then—I admit it—I pulled a Greg Gossip. I drove by the Lake Michigan Inn before I went back to the office. I just wanted to see if Rhett's car was in the parking lot. And it was. A white Cadillac Escalade with an Illinois tag, the same one I'd seen parked at the Dome Home. Had Rhett managed to make a new friend in Warner Pier? Or had he imported a friend from Chicago?

I laughed, but then I noticed another car in the lot, a dark Buick sedan, also with an Illinois tag. It made me remember the two guys in city coats who had been in Hogan's office the night Derrick Valentine was killed.

Was that their car? Or did it belong to someone else? Were they staying at the Lake Michigan Inn? Somehow I hadn't had the feeling they'd be around that long. Who were they, anyway? Joe knew. Had he gone to the Lake Michigan Inn to see them? Why wouldn't he tell me?

My curiosity bump was itching furiously.

I drove to the shop, and I tried to put the whole thing out of my mind. Then, for the first time all day, I got to work. For about an hour I churned it out, concentrating on paying bills for TenHuis Chocolade.

I was still concentrating when someone knocked at the door.

After I'd gulped three times to get my heart out of my throat and back down into my chest, I decided to ignore the knock. After all, we weren't open for business.

Of course, it would be quite obvious to passersby that someone was there. Although shades covered our big show windows, I'd turned on the lights in the shop and in my office. Somehow I hadn't wanted any shadows. And those lights would be leaking around the edges of the window shades.

But my plan to refuse to open up went by the way when the person outside began to rattle the door handle.

What if the person at the door broke in?

My heart was back up in my mouth. The shop isn't exactly as secure as Fort Knox. Two years earlier, we'd been hit by a burglar who had simply kicked in the long glass panel in the front door and walked through. Since then we'd acquired an alarm system, but there was nothing to stop someone from getting in before the cops could respond.

Should I call the police? What would I tell them? A customer came to the door after hours, and I was too scared to even see who it was?

It might be someone I knew.

I took my cell phone from my purse and punched in 9-1-1. With my finger over the button that would send the call on its way, I went to the front door.

I turned on the outside lights. Then I yanked at the roller shade and sent it flying up to the top of the window. It made a clatter that made me jump. But I peered through the window, faking calm annoyance and holding my cell phone, with my finger ready to hit the call button, in plain view.

I yelled, "We're not open!"

Between the light from the shop and the streetlight two doors down, I could see the man standing there fairly clearly.

It was the hulking guy who had gone into the Dock Street Pizza Place as Joe and I were leaving.

He yelled back at me, "I need to talk to you!"

"Come back tomorrow!"

I pulled the blind back down. Then I waited, phone in hand, to see if he shattered the glass in the door.

He didn't. Instead, after a moment I heard footsteps crunching as he walked away. Car lights bounced off our windows, and I heard a car drive off.

I felt weak all over as I went back to my desk. Before I left for home, I vowed, I would call the police dispatcher and ask that the lone night shift patrolman be sent to stand by as I opened that door to dash for my van.

I considered the man at the door. What had he wanted? Why was he so eager to talk to someone at TenHuis Chocolade that he had come at nine o'clock at night, rather than waiting until we were open the next day?

Who was he?

A memory tickled my brain. I reached into the file folder I had assembled on Christina Meachum. I pulled out the picture of her husband, Harold Belcher. Belcher the Butcher.

Chapter 11

It was only nine o'clock. I called Hogan.

After the usual sorry-to-bother-you remarks, I told him about the strange man who had come to the door.

"I feel stupid about this, Hogan, but I told you that I had looked Christina Meachum up on the Internet and found out she was the ex-wife of Harold Belcher."

"Belcher the Butcher."

"Right. I printed out a picture of Harold. It's several years old, of course, but looking at that picture—well, the guy at the door could have been him."

Hogan didn't say anything.

I went on. "It definitely was not the guy you and Joe were talking to last night."

"Why did you think of him?"

"Because if you described the two men, you'd use the same words. Big nose. Ugly. Bald. But the man who came to the door was not the same person. To begin with, he had hair around the edges of his scalp. He didn't shave his head all over, the way your guy does."

Hogan gave a grunt. "Don't call him 'my guy.' He's nothing to me but a pain in the neck. Are you going to be at the shop for a few more minutes?"

"I'm almost ready to leave. I admit I was thinking of calling Joe and asking him to drive down and escort me to my van."

"Wait there. I need to talk to you. Then I'll follow you home."

Hogan was at the door in less than ten minutes. He knocked and called out my name, and I let him in.

"I'm probably being silly," I said. "Probably the guy was looking for directions, and mine was the only light he saw."

"No. I'm glad you called. If there's a chance Harold Belcher is in town, I want to know about it. I already passed the word on to the State Police. Not that we can do anything."

"Why not?"

"If what I read in the paper is right, Belcher is out on bond. As far as I know, he can go anywhere he wants to, at least in the state of Michigan, as long as he behaves himself. But if he's in my area, I'd prefer to keep an eye on him. I wanted to talk to you about something different."

"Sure. Come in the office and sit down." I led the way to my glassed-in room.

Hogan took off his jacket and hat and sat in the one visitor's chair. "It's Nettie. She's having some sort of nervous crisis, and she won't tell me what's wrong. So I'm asking you. What's going on with her?"

I think I kept from giving a guilty start, but I cleared my throat before I spoke. "She found a dead man in the alley last night. That might be preying on her mind."

"No. She talks about that readily. It gives her the willies, but she's coping. This is something different, something she doesn't want to tell me." Hogan gave me a long, level stare. "I thought you might know what it was."

I blinked dully, wondering how to react.

Hogan pressed his point. "Do you know what's wrong, Lee?"

"I'm trying to thick. I mean, think! Give me a minute."

Quandary with a capital Q. Of course, probably what Aunt Nettie was upset about was keeping quiet about Pamela—Pamela who turned out to be Christina and who had left in the middle of the night with Myrl. We both felt guilty about not telling Hogan her real identity. But Aunt Nettie's best friend was determined that Myrl's name must not appear in this, no matter what. So that left Aunt Nettie—and me— between the proverbial rock and the equally proverbial hard place.

Aunt Nettie wasn't going to be happy with me if I blabbed to Hogan about Pamela. I sighed. "I'm sorry. I can't tell you a thing."

He leaned back in his chair and eyed me casually. I remembered uneasily that over his forty years in law enforcement Hogan had interviewed hundreds of unwilling witnesses. My face began to feel hot.

"Seems as if a whole bunch of folks are disappearing around here," he said.

"Success? I mean—Such as?" Now I'd done it. My tongue had twisted twice, and Hogan would know that meant I was nervous. "Who's disappeared?"

"That detective who came to see you. The second guy."

"O'Sullivan? I thought the State Police had hauled him in."

"Nope. He fled the scene before they got to him."

"Doesn't that show that he feels guilty?"

"We all feel guilty about something. He's probably headed back to Georgia. They'll pick him up. I'm more concerned about that woman who disappeared."

I made my voice as innocent as possible. "What woman?"

"Some woman who worked here in the shop. Nettie won't tell me anything about her."

"Then how did you know she disappeared?"

"Joe let it out. He said you'd been up and down last night because some woman came to the house, slept a few hours, then left."

"Oh," I said. We both sat silently for a few minutes.

Hogan finally spoke. "So, Lee, who was this woman?"

I sighed. "She was a temporary employee named Pamela Thompson. She had been having family problems. She called Aunt Nettie last night—while you were busy investigating Derrick Valentine's death—and told her she thought the guy she was afraid of had found her."

"Who was this guy?"

"Her ex-husband, I think. Anyway, Aunt Nettie met her at the Shell station out on the highway and brought her to our house."

"Why didn't she bring her to our place?"

"You'll have to ask Aunt Nettie that one. But I think it was because she thought whoever was looking for Pamela would be less likely to find her at our house."

"Where did this Pamela Thompson go?"

"I don't know, Hogan. She had contacted a friend, and someone showed up to get her about five thirty this morning."

"Who picked her up?"

"I'd never seen the woman before, and Pamela didn't introduce us." That wasn't exactly a lie. I went on hurriedly. "All I know is that Pamela went willingly."

Hogan kept looking at me. I knew he was trying to get me to add to my story. I was determined that I wouldn't do that.

After about two minutes of silence, Hogan won. I spoke. "Hogan, I don't see how Pamela could have had anything to do with Derrick Valentine's death. She never spoke to him. He never saw her. They had no contact."

Hogan rubbed his eyes with both heels of his hands. He looked exhausted.

"I guess I'm getting tunnel vision," he said. "It's just that we have this dead detective. Then we have this missing detective. Then there's this missing woman. Then we have the Marson Endicott bunch nagging us over their missing woman. Who turns up on CNN, so I guess she's not missing anymore. And now you think Harold Belcher may be in town."

He gave a deep sigh. "It's a regular crime wave. And with all these things happening at the same time in a town this small, it seems as if they should fit together."

"What could Pamela—a woman willing to take a temporary job doing unskilled work in a chocolate shop—have to do with a high flier like Marson Endicott?"

"Beats me." He stood up. "You ready to go?"

"Let me call Joe and tell him I'm on the way."

"Yeah. It'd be dumb to get escorted to your vehicle here on the main street, then run through the deep, dark woods to get into your house."

I gathered up the last bit of work I'd hoped to accomplish—comparing the phone bill to my own record of long distance calls—and stuck my computer flash drive in my pocket. Now that you can load a mass of information on a gadget five-eighths of an inch by two and three-eighths inches, I try to take it home automatically, so that I can work at home if I need to.

Hogan escorted me to my van; then he followed me home. He pulled into the drive behind me, said, "Hello," when Joe came out to meet us, and declined an invitation to come in.

He drove away leaving me mired in guilt so deep I could hardly walk into the house. I was longing to tell him the whole story, not the carefully expurgated version I'd handed out. I felt terrible. Hogan treated me almost like a daughter. He had been wonderful to me and to Joe.

Plus, he was a highly professional law officer. He might be able to use the information I was keeping to myself.

But I couldn't say anything without getting Sarajane's approval. I simply could not threaten the carefully built structure of her underground railroad.

I decided to make one more effort at getting Sarajane's permission to tell Hogan the real story about Pamela-Christina.

Joe went back to some basketball game he'd been watching, and I went into the bedroom and called Sarajane. I nearly fell off the bed when a man answered.

"Good evening! Peach Street Bed-and-Breakfast!"

A man? Answering Sarajane's phone?

I was even more surprised when I recognized the voice. "Rhett?"

His voice dropped almost to a whisper. "P.J., what are you doing calling this number? Listen, I'm taking care of this end."

"Rhett?"

He kept whispering. "I'll call you on my cell. It may be an hour or so."

Then he hung up.

I stared at the phone. That was the oddest phone call I'd ever taken part in.

For a moment I wondered if I'd called the right number. Then I remembered; Rhett had answered with "Peach Street Bed-and-Breakfast." Yes, I had called Sarajane's number, though I had no idea why Rhett answered it.

I began to laugh. Who did Rhett think I was? Obviously someone he didn't want to talk to at the moment. That left a lot of possibilities, of course. It could be the person who ate the second pizza. It could be some business contact he was trying to dodge. Maybe it was someone he owed money. But I really couldn't see any reason why it would be me.

In fact, he'd said a name. Or rather initials. "P.J." They meant nothing to me.

I still needed to talk to Sarajane. I hit redial.

Rhett answered again. "Peach Street Bed-and-Breakfast."

This time I started with my name. "It's Lee Woodyard, Rhett. I wanted to talk to Sarajane."

Rhett gasped, then spoke. "Mrs. Woodyard? Did you call a moment ago?"

"Yep."

"I'm so sorry I hung up. I thought you were someone else."

"That's what I figured. What are you doing at Sarajane's?"

"I'm helping out with computer problems. We stuck Mrs. Harding with three of our guys, and one of them is having trouble checking his e-mail."

"He'll continue to have problems," I said. "Warner Pier is still in the dark ages computer-wise. No wireless service."

"I have a direct satellite link, so I brought my laptop over for him to use."

"Where's Sarajane?"

"Mrs. Harding is preparing bedtime snacks. She asked me to get the phone because she was halfway up the stairs with a tray of cheese, fruit, and cookies. Shall I have her call you back?"

At that point I heard a voice roar in the background. The roar faded to a rumble almost immediately, and I deduced that Rhett had put his hand over the receiver, blocking the sound. But I had caught three words, none of them fit to be used in polite company.

Poor Sarajane, I thought. Potty Mouth was one of her guests.

In thirty seconds or so Rhett was back on the line. "Sorry," he said. "I had to take care of a problem."

"Who is that guy?" I asked.

"Whom do you mean?"

"Potty Mouth. He was swearing at the television set this morning."

"I believe you're referring to Mr. Smith. Elliot J. Smith. Mr. Smith is chief financial officer of the Prodigal Corporation."

I made a disgusted noise. "I can't believe a man that crude has reached the upper echelons of an important corporation."

"Oh, yes, it's true." Rhett's voice was amused.

"You must have an extremely varied set of duties."

"Yes, Mr. Smith is regarded as a financial genius. I think Mrs. Harding will be here shortly. Do you want to hold?"

"He's standing there, right? And he's mad because his e-mail won't behave."

"That is correct."

"Tell Sarajane I'll be up until midnight, and it's important that I talk to her."

We hung up.

I had learned one interesting thing. Potty Mouth was Elliot J. Smith. He'd been mentioned often in the articles about the Prodigal scandal.

Elliot J. Smith had a lot to swear about, according to the newspapers and magazines. If the charges of financial manipulation being lodged against Marson Endicott were substantiated, the chief financial officer of Prodigal was in serious trouble. There's no way he could have failed to know what was going on unless he hadn't been to the office in a couple of years.

I decided I might as well get into something comfortable. As I put on my emerald green velvet robe—the one Joe gave me—I thought over my conversation with Rhett. It still seemed odd for him to be at Sarajane's, despite his responsibilities for tending to the needs of all the members of Marson Endicott's business conference.

But Rhett hadn't simply been surprised by my first call, when he'd mistaken me for someone else; he'd been annoyed, or even alarmed. And what was he taking care of? As in, "I'm taking care of things at this end."

Again I wondered who P.J. was. She could have been calling from anywhere in the world, not just from Warner Pier, but maybe the call was from his fellow pizza eater.

And just who was that?

And, I asked myself, was the identity of Rhett's pizza pal any of my business? The answer was no.

I had zipped up my robe and picked up the phone bill I needed to go over when Sarajane called back.

She sounded harried. "Lee. What's up?"

"I need to talk to you seriously, Sarajane, so if this isn't a good time . . ."

"No. I think I have everybody settled. Thanks to Rhett."

"He seems to be the go-to guy for that bunch at the Dome Home."

"He's been a godsend to me. He came over last night, explained exactly who would be staying here, and what each man would need. He's even giving them breakfast tomorrow. Now, what can I do for you?"

I steeled myself for an argument. "Sarajane, you've left Aunt Nettie in a bad spot over Pamela, and I'm not sure how much longer she can go on without telling Hogan who Pamela really was and who took her away."

I expected a huge protest. Instead, I got silence.

I went on. "I'm not kidding. You know Aunt Nettie's about as sneaky as—well, as sneaky as a brass band in full marching regalia, with cymbals."

"Yes, I know."

"Tonight Hogan began on me. He knows she's hiding something, and he wants to know what it is. He's going to keep asking her. How long do you think she can hold out?"

"About a minute."

"Right. Aunt Nettie is simply going to have to tell him about Pamela. Wouldn't it be better if you told him?"

Sarajane gave a deep sigh. "I'm afraid you're right, Lee."

It was my turn to give a deep sigh. Of relief. "Sarajane, I'm sure that's the thing to do."

"Can we wait until morning?"

"Actually, Hogan went home less than an hour ago, and he seemed completely exhausted. I think waiting until morning is an excellent idea."

"Maybe by then Myrl and Pamela will have turned up."

"Turned up? I thought they called in early this afternoon."

"They did. Or Pamela did. But . . ."

"But what?"

"Myrl always calls her mother at eight p.m. every night. No matter where she is. And tonight she didn't call."

Chapter 12

I couldn't comprehend Sarajane's words.

"Let me get this straight," I said. "Myrl still hasn't let anyone know where she and Pamela are?"

"Oh, yes. The person she called didn't tell me where they are, of course, but apparently Myrl contacted—well, the right person, the person who needs to know."

"Then they're okay?"

"As far as I can tell. It's just that skipping the phone call to her mother was an odd thing for Myrl to do."

"Maybe we should talk to Hogan tonight, Sarajane."

"No. I feel sure they're safe. Let Hogan get his sleep."

We left it at that, but I wasn't happy.

I moved my papers to the dining table and tried to concentrate on reconciling the telephone bill. I've been picky about this since one of our employees ran up the bill one month by repeatedly calling her boyfriend in Muskegon. Since then I log all my long-distance calls on a pad I keep beside the telephone, and I request that everyone else do the same thing.

Of course, I wouldn't swear I never forget to write a call down, but logging it in has become second nature to me. Aunt Nettie and her chief assistant, Dolly Jolly, also occasionally make calls, and I've nagged until they rarely forget to log either. Besides, most of the people we call—our customers and suppliers—are on our phone bill month after month. I recognize their numbers and know why someone would have called them. So reconciling the phone bill is normally a ten-minute chore.

But this time I came up with two numbers I didn't recognize, numbers that also weren't listed on the log.

My earlier suspicion that Pamela had called someone from the TenHuis phone flashed through my mind.

One of the numbers had the same area code as a Chicago gift shop we supplied with seasonal chocolate, but I knew it hadn't been made to that store. They had a number that ended by spelling out g-i-f-t, so it ended with 4-4-3-8.

The second unlogged number had an area code I didn't recognize, 7-7-0.

Could Pamela have made the calls?

I could fire up the computer and try reverse lookup, but my home computer connects to the Internet very slowly—one effect of living in a small town that isn't electronically up-to-date. We have a satellite connection at the office, but Joe and I are still in the dark ages of dial-up at home.

Or I could use my cell phone and simply call the numbers and see who answered. I had plenty of minutes to do that at no extra charge. But my cell phone might not be working. Thanks to its location on the edge of a big lake and away from larger cities, Warner Pier has huge dead zones. Sometimes we can use a cell phone at our house, and sometimes we can't. Sometimes it helps to go upstairs, but I'm sure there's no service from our basement.

I reached for the cell phone, and the little marks went up

on its tiny screen, showing that I had at least minimal service. It was after ten o'clock, late to be making phone calls, but— tough. I wanted to get through with that phone bill, and I wanted to know if Pamela had used the office phone. I decided I'd try the two numbers. The unknown area code was probably in a time zone west of us, I told myself, so it would be earlier wherever it was. The Chicago number was an hour earlier, I knew. We're Eastern; Chicago is Central.

So I first punched in the 7-7-0 number. It picked up on the second ring. But it was a recording that merely asked me to leave a message. It didn't identify the person or business who paid the phone bill. My caller ID simply showed the number.

I hung up. I'd have to call again in the daytime.

Next I tried the Chicago number. The phone rang four times before it was picked up. As soon as I said hello, a voice spoke tersely. "You bitch," it said.

It was a gruff, raspy voice—what my grandmother would have called a whiskey voice. It sounded so rough that for a moment, I almost decided not to go on.

I did speak, however. "I beg your pardon!"

The voice rasped again. "I'm not in the mood for jokes." Then the line went dead.

So much for that effort. I hung up. I must have made a disgusted noise, because Joe put the television set on mute and turned around. "What's wrong?"

"I just called someone rude. Or maybe I was rude."

He looked puzzled. "You're not usually rude. Who'd you call?"

"I don't know."

"If you don't know them, why did you call?"

I explained about the unidentified number, though I didn't

go into its possible connection to Pamela. "So I thought I'd take a shortcut and call the numbers," I said.

"Did the rude guy's name come up on your caller ID?"

"Nope. Just a number. Unfortunately, he'll see my name and number on his caller ID. So he'll know who called him. Unless . . ." I quickly checked my phone. "Oh, thank goodness! My outgoing calls are blocked. He won't know who called. We can start fresh tomorrow. I have to call the other number then anyway. Or check the reverse directory."

Joe frowned. "Then you were trying to identify two numbers?"

"Right."

"When were the calls made?"

I double-checked the dates. "Both the same day. Two weeks ago. They were the final calls made during the billing period."

"And you don't know who's at the other number?"

"No. I'll try again tomorrow. I don't even know where the area code is."

"We might be able to figure it out from the phone book."

Joe brought the telephone directory and found the page with a map of area codes. He traced them down, starting at the top right with New England. I would have given up, but he hung in there, reading the tiny numbers as his fingers followed the East Coast.

Finally he tapped the page. "Huh! It's an Atlanta prefix."

"Atlanta? Surely not Atlanta!"

"Do you know anybody in Atlanta?"

I thought before I spoke. "Just one person, Joe."

"Who's that? A customer?"

"No, I don't think we have any regular customers in Atlanta. The only people from there I've met recently were Derrick Valentine and Tom O'Sullivan of PDQ Investigations."

"Whoops!"

I nodded. "Joe, could somebody have used our office phone to call PDQ Investigations in Atlanta? Two weeks ago?"

"It doesn't seem likely. Maybe one of the ladies called her Aunt Millie in Smyrna."

"I think I can check it out." I reached for my purse and dumped out the collection of notes, business cards, and scraps of paper that had accumulated in the side pocket. Sure enough, Tom O'Sullivan's card was among the junk.

I read the number off. It was two digits away from the number that had been called from the TenHuis telephone.

If a company, such as a detective agency, signed up for several phone numbers to be used by employees, it would be logical for the numbers to be consecutive. So I thought it likely that the call from our phone had been to PDQ Investigations.

"Who would have called them?" Joe said.

"I have a vague idea," I said. "Let me think about it."

The truth was, PDQ Investigations had undoubtedly already told the Michigan State Police who hired them to come to Warner Pier. Underwood or Hogan would know if it were likely that Pamela had called PDQ.

I stood up. "I'm going to bed. I can't think about this anymore tonight. It's too weird."

But of course I did think about it. I went to bed, and I slept. But Derrick Valentine and PDQ Investigations haunted me. The last time I woke up, the lighted dial on my bedside clock said four forty-nine.

"Groan," I said. Then I turned over and went back to sleep

until seven, when I realized that Joe was on his feet and dressed. "I'm meeting a guy for breakfast," he said. "See you tonight."

He gave me a kiss, but by the time I was awake enough to realize he was leaving, it was too late to ask where he was going.

I turned off the alarm and lay there, trying to wake up and anticipating what the day was to bring.

The first thing, of course, was the confession session with Hogan, when Aunt Nettie, Sarajane, and I would have to admit we'd helped Pamela flee Warner Pier before she could be questioned about the death of the private detective who had come looking for her.

And how about the mysterious phone call to Atlanta? All I could think to do about the situation was to add it to the list of things to discuss with Hogan. At seven thirty I had him on the phone, arranging to meet with him, Aunt Nettie, and Sarajane at nine at the Peach Street B&B. If Sarajane's guests were going out to the Dome Home for breakfast, she should be free by that time. I called her, but I didn't ask if we could come. I simply said we'd be there.

Thinking of Pamela brought another question to mind. And that was the identity of the big ugly man who had rattled the TenHuis Chocolade door the previous evening. Was he, as I suspected, Harold "the Butcher" Belcher? But if so, how had he known that his ex-wife had any connection with TenHuis Chocolade?

Unless he was the one who'd hired PDQ Investigations—

But then why had his ex-wife called PDQ Investigations? *If* she was the one who had made the phone calls.

And if Pamela had called the private detective agency, why

hadn't she said so? When Aunt Nettie, Sarajane, and I carefully shielded her from being seen by Derrick Valentine, why hadn't she said, "Oh, I hired him myself?" Or, "He's my uncle." Or something.

I was more confused than ever as I headed for the Peach Street B&B. This wasn't going to be a pleasant morning.

My expectation was confirmed when I saw a car turn into the B&B's driveway ahead of me. It might not have an official insignia on it, but the black buzz cut behind the steering wheel told me it was driven by State Police Lieutenant Larry Underwood. I'd run into him before. He was a conscientious officer, but no Mr. Personality. Underwood must be the State Police officer in charge of the investigation into Derrick Valentine's death.

Hogan had apparently asked him to join our confession session. Talking to the two of them was going to be a lot harder than talking to Hogan on his own.

But we managed. Hogan and Aunt Nettie arrived just after I did. We all went into Sarajane's kitchen, where she furnished us with coffee, and Sarajane, Aunt Nettie, and I told our story. I was only glad that they didn't separate us and go for serious interrogations.

Sarajane was the star storyteller, of course. She came clean about Pamela Thompson's true identity as Christina Meachum and explained that Aunt Nettie and I had agreed to help the fugitive ex–Mrs. Belcher earn a little money during the two or three weeks she was to be forced to stay in Warner Pier. Sarajane went on about how she got out of the shower to find Pamela in a panic because someone had phoned the house and called her by name. Pamela, she said, had answered the phone thinking it was a call from Aunt Nettie. Sarajane doesn't use caller ID.

Aunt Nettie told about picking up Pamela—who was really Christina—at the Shell station and stashing her at our house. I described how Myrl Sawyer came for her at five in the morning. Sarajane reported the phone call she'd had from Pamela later, saying that she and Myrl had reached a safe place.

Underwood carefully took Sarajane over the evening of Valentine's death, making sure Sarajane could vouch for Pamela's whereabouts for the whole evening. Sarajane said she had met Pamela around five forty-five, after Pamela parked George Jenkins' van in the alley behind his art gallery. They had waited in Sarajane's van until Aunt Nettie dropped George off and gave Pamela her coat. Then they had driven straight back to the B&B. Sarajane had started preparing dinner.

But at six fifteen Rhett Spivey showed up. "I had to quit cooking and go over things with him," Sarajane said. "I was housing three of the Prodigal executives beginning the next night."

Underwood was taking notes of everything she said. "Did Pamela Thompson talk with Spivey?"

"No, when he rang the doorbell she made herself scarce. We were careful about her meeting people. We'd already arranged that if the doorbell rang, she was to go into her room."

"Where was her room?"

"On the ground floor. Down the hall off the kitchen. It's part of my apartment. We wanted to keep her separate from any guests."

Underwood nodded. "So she didn't participate in the meeting with Spivey?"

"No. I think she spent the time packing; we knew she'd have to leave. Her television set was on, the way it always was." Sarajane sighed. "Pamela was one of these people who can't stand silence. She always wanted the TV on, even if it was just the Styles Channel or something like that. I think she did a load of laundry, too. She couldn't have gone anywhere. She didn't have a car."

"Where was your car?"

"In the garage. I had the car keys in my pocket. I keep them attached to my house keys."

"How long was Spivey there?"

"Oh, I thought he'd never leave! He went over every little detail—what kind of towels those men liked, what sort of bedtime snacks, what blend of coffee. You'd think he was the only person in the world who knew how to handle guests. It was helpful, I suppose, but I wasn't in the mood."

Yes, that sounded like Rhett, the Butler. He was a freak on details. I felt sorry for Sarajane. She'd had a crisis going on with Pamela, and she'd been forced to stop and deal with Rhett. He was lucky she wasn't the murdering kind. I would have been tempted to shove him down the stairs.

After Underwood had quizzed Sarajane thoroughly, establishing that there was no way Pamela could have left the B&B, I brought up the mysterious phone calls made from the Ten-Huis phone. I repeated all my questions about them. Yes, I agreed, Pamela was probably physically present at the time they were made. But why? What connection would she have had with PDQ Investigations? If they were helping her ex-husband, PDQ representatives would be the last people she'd want to contact.

"There's a lot I don't understand about all this," I said, "but one thing is sure. Pamela had no contact with Derrick Valentine. Sarajane, Aunt Nettie, and I all worked hard to make sure she didn't. So I do not see how she could be concerned in his death."

"Neither do I," Underwood said. He thanked us politely for our information and told us not to leave town. Then he sat back quietly, leaving it to Hogan to scold us. Which Hogan did.

"You've impeded an important investigation by at least twenty-four hours," he said. "Three normally law-abiding women. I'm ashamed of you."

We all acted properly contrite.

When he was through, I spoke. "The main thing I'm worried about is Myrl Sawyer and Pamela." I turned to Sarajane. "Have they checked in again with Myrl's supervisor—if she has one?"

"No." Sarajane looked miserable. "I'm terribly worried about them."

"We'll get the full license plate number for Myrl's car," Underwood said. "We'll have people looking for them within half an hour."

"But they could be anywhere!" Sarajane said. "They've been gone more than twenty-four hours. They could be clear across the country."

Underwood didn't have anything comforting to say to that.

I was relieved when he and Hogan stood up. I was ready for this uncomfortable interview to be over.

But Sarajane raised her hand like a timid third grader. "Just one more thing."

"What's that?" Hogan's voice was brusque.

"Hogan, do you remember that I came by the station and picked up the papers so I could get a license to carry a firearm?"

"Yes, I remember. You took the class up at Holland, didn't you?"

"Yes. And I practice regularly—every week at the Warner County Gun Association firing range."

"All perfectly legal, Sarajane. What's the problem?"

She pleated her paper napkin, making it into a little fan. "Well . . ."

"Well, what?"

"Ever since yesterday morning I've been looking for that pistol."

Hogan didn't say anything, and Sarajane looked up with anguished eyes.

"Hogan, my pistol is not where it's supposed to be. I can't find it anywhere in the house!"

Chocolate Chat
Parts of the Cacao Bean

"Nibs" is the name given to the cacao seeds, or beans. The nibs must go through four basic steps before they become chocolate liquor, the term used for pure chocolate.

"Fermentation" is a process that removes the pulp that surrounds the nibs when they are removed from the pod. During fermentation the seeds germinate, then are killed by high temperatures.

"Drying" follows, with the beans losing as much as half their weight as moisture is removed.

"Roasting" comes next. This takes more than an hour at temperatures of 94 to 104 degrees Fahrenheit.

"Winnowing" removes a thin, useless shell.

Now the beans are ready to be ground into that precious "cacao liquor."

From here on the product is chocolate.

Chapter 13

Hogan's voice was calm. "Do you think this Pamela took the pistol?"

"I don't know what to think," Sarajane said. "I only know that it's not in either of the two places where I keep it. Or anywhere else. I've torn the house apart."

"You're not a forgetful person, Sarajane. So that sounds as if it's gone. Pamela could have taken it."

"But why? Why would Pamela take my pistol?"

I made an impatient noise. "If I'd been in her position, I might have taken it. She was already fleeing for her life. Then a private detective showed up at her place of employment, looking for her. Next someone called the house where she was staying, again looking for her. I would have taken a cannon if one had been available."

"Why didn't she tell me she was taking it?" Sarajane said.

Hogan answered. "Because she thought you'd say no. But let's not get excited. We can understand Pamela wanting to have a pistol for protection. She's not likely to start holding up banks or gunning people down in the street."

Hogan zipped up his jacket, and I asked one final question

before he could leave. "What do I do if Belcher shows up at the shop again?"

"He won't." Underwood answered, and he made his reply sound final. "We found out where he's staying. We'll talk to him."

"But you can't arrest him?"

"Not as things stand at the present. But we can make him aware that we know he's here, and we're keeping an eye on him. At any rate, no matter who tries to talk to you about Pamela or Christina or whoever she is, don't say a word."

I had to be satisfied with that. Aunt Nettie told Hogan he could go on, and she joined me in the van as I left for the shop.

I buckled up securely. "Whew!" I said. "I'm glad that's over."

Aunt Nettie laughed. "I agree. I feel a whole lot better since I've been honest with Hogan."

"There's nothing like a clear conscience to give you a good day. And I particularly liked the reassurance that they're dealing with Harold Belcher."

We drove down Peach Street, leaving Sarajane's B&B behind us at the edge of town, passing through a neighborhood of lovely old Victorian houses, and arriving in Warner Pier's quaint redbrick business district. I turned onto Fifth Street and pulled into a parking place in front of the shop.

"Maybe Belcher the Butcher will go back to Detroit," I said.

"The headline will be: 'Big-city gangster vanquished by small-town cop,' " Aunt Nettie said.

We were both laughing as we went into the shop. And there, standing by the cash register, was a big, ugly, bald guy I had seen before.

My insides whirled around, but I guess all I did was stare. I was trying to convince myself this big, ugly guy was the chief financial officer of the Prodigal Corporation, Elliot J. Smith.

But he wasn't. This one had a fringe of hair over his ears. He was Harold—the Butcher—Belcher.

Belcher's gray jacket with the yellow stripes was draped over the back of one of the two chairs we keep in the retail area. He had apparently been watching for us through the show window and had stood up as we approached.

He wasn't brandishing a blackjack, aiming a gat, or doing anything else threatening. He wasn't biting his nails, tapping his foot, or doing anything that indicated he was nervous. He was simply there, looking like an ordinary customer.

He addressed Aunt Nettie. "Mrs. Jones, I need some help."

Aunt Nettie could never resist an appeal like that one. She smiled. "Of course. What can I do for you?"

I realized that Aunt Nettie didn't recognize Belcher. She thought he was an ordinary customer. I had never shown her the pictures I'd taken from the Internet.

What had happened to Hogan and Lieutenant Underwood's plan to keep Belcher away from us? And what should I do about it? Scream? Fall in a faint? Call the cops? Run out the door and down the street?

Before I could decide, Belcher was speaking again.

"I'm Harold Belcher," he said. "I'm looking for my wife, Christina. I thought you might know where she is."

Aunt Nettie blinked twice and gave a little gasp, but she didn't lose her aplomb. "Oh, my," she said. "I can't help you."

I decided I had to match Aunt Nettie's matter-of-fact attitude. "We've been instructed by the police not to discuss this matter," I said.

"What matter?"

"The death of Derrick Valentine."

"What does . . . ?" Belcher stopped. He took a deep breath before he went on. "I heard on the TV that someone was killed here. But what does that have to do with Christina?"

"I don't know," Aunt Nettie said gently. "But the investigators have told us not to talk about anything at all. Why don't you ask them if there's a connection?"

Belcher gave a bland, smooth smile. "I'm afraid they're not likely to tell me anything. But I think you misunderstand the situation, Mrs. Jones. Everybody thinks I'm out to hurt Christina. But that's not true. I just need to talk to her about a legal matter. She's left me in difficulties with this disappearing act."

I was surprised by Belcher's language and behavior. He looked like a thug, true, but he didn't act like one.

"I'm sorry," Aunt Nettie said. She sounded sorry, and I'm sure she was. "But I don't know anything about where your ex-wife is, and if I did, the investigating officers have told me not to discuss anything with anybody. So I can't help. Please approach the authorities. I'm sure they could assist you."

Belcher smiled again. I was becoming fascinated with his reactions. No matter what Aunt Nettie said, he smiled. He was giving the impression of a genuinely friendly concern for the ex-wife who had sent him to prison.

In other words, his behavior was strange.

Now he spoke coaxingly. "I'm sure you could help me find Christina, Mrs. Jones."

"I'm afraid I can't, Mr. Belcher."

"Can't? Or won't?" His smile was still friendly.

"Talk to the authorities." Aunt Nettie's voice was sweet, but it was firm.

Belcher kept smiling, but something changed. His smile seemed to harden, to set. Maybe like a cement overcoat. Now it didn't look friendly. It looked threatening.

"It's vital that I find Christina," he said. "Vital. A lot depends on it."

Aunt Nettie was still calm. "Please talk to the law enforcement authorities."

The situation wasn't getting anywhere. I'd gotten over my first fright at realizing we were confronting the infamous Belcher the Butcher. But he kept asking the same question, and Aunt Nettie kept giving him the same answer.

I guess I became impatient with the quiet back-and-forth he and Aunt Nettie were trading. Anyway, I jumped into the conversation. "We're not getting anywhere, Mr. Belcher. I suggest that you leave."

Belcher's face flared red, and for a moment I thought he was going to lose his quiet demeanor. He took two steps toward Aunt Nettie and me, stopping just an arm's length away from us.

"I guess you're this Mrs. Woodyard I heard about," he said. "You could answer my question."

I don't know if I was frightened or angry, but I'd had enough. "No. You answer mine, Mr. Belcher. Why are you here?"

"I'm looking for my wife."

"Your ex-wife, right? But what in blazes makes you think that either my aunt or I has any idea on God's green earth where she is?"

He laughed.

"We don't," I said firmly. "And if we did, we've been instructed by the police not to tell anybody anything. So please leave."

He raised his eyebrows. "Without my chocolate?"

"What chocolate?"

"The lady who came up to help me is fixing me up a special box of those cute little cherubs." Now his smile became sarcastic. "Don't tell me you don't want my money."

"Please be seated." I took off my jacket. "Aunt Nettie, perhaps you'd better check on the workroom."

"I'll find out about the cupids," she said. I thought she looked a bit relieved as she moved toward the back of the shop.

I tried to act as if confronting a gangster was the way I started every workday. I went into my office—the door was standing open—and hung my coat on the hall tree in the corner. I went behind the counter and checked the cash register to see if we'd had any earlier sales.

While I was doing that, Belcher seated himself again. In a few minutes one of the hairnet ladies—the geniuses who actually make our bonbons, truffles, and molded chocolate—brought me a white cardboard box marked with the TenHuis Chocolade logo. "He asked for three large and a dozen small cupids," she said. "Assorted flavors."

I peeked inside to check the order. Then I tied a red Valentine ribbon around the box and added a TenHuis card and a gold cupid. I told Harold Belcher the price, and he produced cash.

Belcher had been silent for five minutes now. He seemed to be cooperating with our request that he leave. Maybe that made me overconfident.

Anyway, I spoke to him, perhaps a bit condescendingly. "Our custom is to give every visitor to our shop a sample truffle or bonbon. Please select anything you like from our display case."

Belcher raised his eyebrows. "Free samples, huh? Now that's interesting."

He put on his jacket, examining the chocolates on display while he did it.

"The dark pyramid is filled with a milky coffee-flavored chocolate," I said. "The dark rectangle with a milk chocolate dot is double fudge. It has layers of milk chocolate and dark chocolate fudge."

Belcher smiled that cold smile again. "I guess I don't need a sample. I have my box of little angels. I'll carry it carefully." He leaned over the counter and stared into my eyes.

"I'd hate it if something bad happened to anything having to do with this shop."

He went out the door without ever losing his smile, the smile that seemed to turn the shop into a deep freeze.

As soon as he was gone Aunt Nettie reappeared. "I called Hogan," she said.

"Thanks. So much for their promise to keep an eye on Belcher the Butcher."

"I hope we've seen the last of him."

"I hope we've seen the last of him *and* his ex-wife. I wish the best for Pamela—or Christina or whatever name she's using now—but I don't want to be mixed up with her anymore."

"She certainly was an inconsiderate employee. The last thing she did was go off with the key to her locker. Unless she gave it to you?"

I groaned and shook my head. "That didn't seem very important to either of us at five thirty yesterday morning. I'll get the master key and make sure the locker is empty. Then I'll have a new key made." I got the master key from my desk drawer and went back to the lockers, located in their own area just off our break room.

TenHuis Chocolade employees are all local women, and as far as I've ever heard, we've never had a case of theft. But it's good business practice to make sure everyone has a private space for her belongings, and that each employee uses that space. Aunt Nettie is quite strict that purses, combs and brushes, and other paraphernalia are kept locked up. Most of the hairnet ladies keep their locker keys on expandable bracelets—the spiral kind that look like old-fashioned telephone cords—that they wear on their upper arms or keep in the pockets of their white smocks. Pamela had had a white bracelet. I recalled seeing it the last afternoon she'd been there.

Heaven knows what would be in her locker. When one of our older employees died unexpectedly, I was astonished at the nature of two paperback books I found when I cleaned out her locker. I didn't return them to her family.

But when I opened Pamela's locker, there was only one item there. It was a spiral bracelet. For a moment I thought Pamela had left her keys in her own locker. But that wouldn't work. First, she couldn't lock the locker if the keys were inside, and second, this bracelet was blue, and I was sure Pamela's had been white.

I picked the bracelet up. Had Pamela had someone else's locker key?

But this bracelet held no keys. The only thing attached to the metal ring was a small charm, a silver Raggedy Ann doll. And the moment I saw that charm, I knew whose keys had been on this bracelet.

I grabbed the bracelet and dashed back through the workroom and to my own desk. I took my own keys out of my purse and unlocked my desk. Then I yanked the top left-hand drawer open.

"Darn!" I said. "Dadgum it to heck." Or I think that was what I said.

Aunt Nettie had followed me. "What's wrong, Lee?"

"Pamela had Dolly's keys!" We stared at each other, completely dismayed.

Dolly Jolly, Aunt Nettie's chief assistant in the chocolate-making end of the business, is a very important friend and business associate to both of us. Dolly is as tall as I am, but broader, and she has bright red hair. She's a talented cook—not only at chocolate, but at nearly everything—and author of a cookbook on Michigan cooking. When she expressed an interest in learning the chocolate business, both Aunt Nettie and I were delighted. Aunt Nettie had even redone the apartment over the TenHuis Chocolade business so that Dolly could live there.

Because she lived right upstairs, Dolly kept more than her locker key on her expandable bracelet. She kept a key to her apartment, so that she could run upstairs if she wished. Because she functioned as assistant manager, she had a key to the shop. And she had a key to a storage area we leased from a neighboring business. Accessed off the alley, it was basically a double garage. Dolly parked her Jeep SUV in one side, and we stored some rarely used pieces of equipment in the other side.

Right at the moment, Dolly was on vacation—two weeks earlier I had personally driven her to Grand Rapids to catch a plane for a month in Florida. And since she was out of town,

Dolly had left me her keys. She had trusted me with them, and I had let her down.

Pamela had snagged them from my drawer—I had no idea when. I also had no idea what Pamela had used them for.

I gnashed my teeth. "Darn Pamela! And darn Dolly!" I said. "I told Dolly she didn't need to leave the keys."

"Why did she leave them? Don't we have another set of keys to her apartment?"

"Sure. I keep them in a lockbox in the bottom drawer. I told Dolly that, but she said we might need to get into the storage room. She said she'd leave them handy. A little too handy!"

I examined the bracelet.

"I don't understand," Aunt Nettie said. "Why would Pamela want Dolly's keys?"

"I don't know. But I'd better check Dolly's apartment and the garage and storage room. I hope she hasn't robbed Dolly—and us!—blind."

I got the master keys out of their locked box in my bottom drawer. Then Aunt Nettie followed as I walked swiftly through the workroom and out the door to the alley. I decided to start by checking the garage. Fear stabbed through me as I put my hand on the door. Should I call Hogan before I opened it?

I thought resolute thoughts, turned the key, and lifted the overhead door.

As daylight entered the dark garage I saw the bumper of a car. But it wasn't the bumper of Dolly's Jeep. I reached for the light switch.

The glaring overhead fixture showed us a gray sedan. The license plate ended in 812

I walked around the side of the car and peeked into the

window. A huddled shape lay across the backseat. For a moment it didn't look like anything but a jacket tossed back there.

Then I saw the dark hair and the earmuffs.

It was Myrl. And I felt sure she was dead.

Chapter 14

Of course, when we found Myrl dead, my immediate expectation was that we'd find Pamela nearby, just as dead. But we didn't.

It wasn't easy telling Hogan we'd found another body. I was glad we didn't have to tell him we'd found two.

Not that Aunt Nettie and I looked for an additional body. Once we'd spotted Myrl lying in the back seat of her car without moving, we backed out, and Aunt Nettie ran for a telephone. I stood in the back door of TenHuis Chocolade until the patrol car got there, but I didn't go into the garage again.

A half hour later, as Aunt Nettie and I sat in my office waiting to talk to the State Police, I was calm enough to make a list of questions about Myrl's death.

Question One was, Had Harold "the Butcher" Belcher killed Myrl? It was easy to think he had intercepted Pamela and Myrl and had killed both of them.

But if that were true, it raised Question Two. If Harold had killed Myrl and Pamela, why hadn't he fled Warner Pier? And that led to Question Three: Why hadn't he left Pamela's body with Myrl's?

And then there was Question Four: If Pamela wasn't dead, where the heck was she?

Question Five was, How could Harold have known about Dolly's garage? The answer to that one was, Pamela would have had to tell him. Question Six—Why on earth would she do that?

As part of an escape plan? Had Pamela managed to escape her murderous ex? Was she now fleeing for her life—on foot in the December snows of Michigan?

Or could she be fleeing in Dolly's car?

Because someone—probably the murderer—had taken Dolly's car out of the alley garage and hidden Myrl's car in its place. So Question Seven was, Where was Dolly's car?

But Pamela didn't have the keys for Dolly's car. Or did she?

After all, we knew that Pamela had had the keys to Dolly's apartment as well as those to her garage. The car keys hadn't been on the key ring Dolly had left in my desk, but Dolly probably had a set of car keys in her apartment someplace.

The situation was terribly confusing, but Harold Belcher still seemed to be the obvious suspect in Myrl's death. And in Pamela's death—if Pamela was dead. But if Harold had killed them, why was he hanging around Warner Pier threatening Aunt Nettie and me?

I'd already written that one down as Question Two, but I considered it again. Could Harold's threats be a ploy to make himself seem innocent? That was pretty far-fetched.

If Harold wasn't guilty, the only alternative would be that Pamela had snapped completely, had herself killed Myrl, and then fled in Dolly's car. That was even more far-fetched.

I threw my pencil down and tried to call Dolly's cell phone. She needed to know that her Jeep was missing and the police were searching her apartment. I could hear them walking around overhead, and I was glad that there was no indication they had found a second body up there. At least they hadn't called for a second ambulance.

I punched in Dolly's cell phone number, but she didn't answer. I left a message on her voice mail, asking her to call me; then I called the hotel where she was staying. She didn't answer, so I left a second message there. I hoped Dolly was frolicking on the beach.

Next I called Joe and had just as much luck reaching him as I had had reaching Dolly. He didn't answer the phone at his shop or the one that should be in his pocket or the one at our house. I didn't try City Hall. If he had been there, someone would have told him Aunt Nettie and I had found another body. He surely would have come over to see about us.

Hogan came into the office to check on Aunt Nettie, and he assured us that law enforcement officers were looking for Dolly's car and that no second body had been found.

Completely frustrated, I opened my computer and began to play Spider. I lost every game.

All work at TenHuis Chocolade had come to a halt. The hairnet ladies were standing in knots gossiping, and Aunt Nettie and I were in the office wringing our hands. I wasn't answering the telephone, and we'd locked the front door.

I'd lost a dozen games of Spider when someone rattled the door handle hard enough that I went to see who it was. When I peeked around the edge of the window blind, I was surprised to see Rhett. I opened the door a crack.

"Hi," he said. "I was sorry to hear you have more problems."

"I'm beginning to feel like the kiss of death. I meet someone for five minutes, and they die."

He looked dismayed. "You knew this person?"

"Not really. Like I said, our paths crossed for five minutes. It's nice of you to come by and sympathize."

"You weren't answering your phone, and I wanted to explain about last night."

Last night? Last night seemed to have happened several months earlier. What was Rhett talking about?

He seemed to realize I was confused. "When I mistook your voice for someone else's," he said.

"Oh! Forget it."

"No, I owe you an apology. I thought you were my obnoxious sister. Your voices are pitched the same."

"That sort of thing happens to all of us. How's the group at the Dome Home?"

"Oh, nothing bothers them." He grinned. "As long as they have chocolate, booze, and cigars. And lawyers. I was concerned about you and your aunt."

I assured him that we were fine, though I wasn't sure that was true.

Then I saw something scary behind him. "Gotta go!" I said. I slammed the door and locked it. I rushed back to Aunt Nettie.

"The TV news team just pulled in."

"Oh, dear," she said.

"Gordon Hitchcock is on the story."

I had bumped heads with Gordon Hitchcock, anchorman for one of the Grand Rapids television stations, earlier that winter. I was not tempted to open the door and speak to him.

Instead I went back to Spider and ignored the banging on the shop's door. I should have been working, but somehow it seemed disrespectful, as if I were thinking, "Oh, gee, another body. Well, I'll call the disposal people and then get back to work." I'm not quite that blasé.

So I played Spider, which takes no brains at all, and mulled over Rhett's visit.

It was nice of him to come by, I thought. Not that he had owed me any explanation for the previous evening's mix-up. He and his sister must not get along. At least he hadn't sounded happy at hearing from her. But she must have known where he was, since she had called the B&B's number. Maybe Rhett had forwarded his calls to that number.

But that wouldn't explain his final comment of the night before. "I said I'd handle this end of things!" Was that what he had said? I was pretty sure that it was. So what "things" were Rhett and his sister involved in? And what was his sister's name? P.J.? Was that what he had called her? It could stand for a lot of things. Patty Jane. Priscilla Jo. Penelope Josepha. Paula Janetta. Patricia Josephine. Pretty Juicy.

I was getting silly. I was ready to think about something else when one of the hairnet ladies ran in and said, "We're on television!"

"What!"

"That Gordon guy. He's broadcasting from outside the shop."

Aunt Nettie and I went back to the break room, where there's a small television set, in time to catch the end of Gordon Hitchcock's report.

"So once again this quaint resort town is in the news. Not

only have two shocking murders occurred, but—in *apparently* unrelated news—the business leader who's at the center of the latest national scandal has taken refuge at his luxurious waterfront mansion here in Warner Pier.

"Yes, Marson Endicott and his legal team are holding strategy meetings . . ."

I tuned him out mentally, shook my head, and went back to my office. As I passed Aunt Nettie, I spoke in disgust. "*Apparently* unrelated? Gordon Hitchcock is really stretching this time. What possible connection could there between a sleazy private detective, an abused wife, and an international financial scandal?"

She smiled. "This too shall pass. I hope without too much more bad publicity for TenHuis Chocolade."

I got to the office to hear the phone ringing again. I saw the number listed on caller ID, and this time I answered. It's not tactful to dodge your mother-in-law's calls.

"Hi, Mercy," I said.

"Oh, Lee, I just got back to the office, and I saw all the commotion over there."

"Commotion?"

"Well, the TV truck. Angie—you know, my new assistant—says there's been another murder!"

"We don't know that it's murder, but it looks likely." I quickly sketched how Aunt Nettie and I had checked out the seldom-used storeroom and discovered a strange car, complete with dead occupant.

"Who was it?"

I paused, wondering how to explain who Myrl was. "A friend of Sarajane Harding's," I said finally.

"In *your* storeroom?"

"It's a long story, Mercy. I don't suppose you've heard from Joe."

"No! I called him to remind him about dinner tonight, and he hadn't returned my call. Lee, something is definitely bothering him."

"You may be right."

"What is it?"

"He's not telling me, Mercy."

"But, Lee . . ."

I was relieved to see Hogan coming through the workroom, headed my way. "Mercy, Hogan's here, and he looks as if he has questions. I'll talk to you later."

I had brushed her off, but I didn't feel guilty. I didn't know what was bugging Joe, and it was best if his mother and I didn't talk about him. Hogan had probably come simply to make sure Aunt Nettie was taking things calmly—the way she usually takes them—but he had given me a good excuse to hang up.

To my surprise Hogan had come to ask Aunt Nettie and me to walk through Dolly's apartment and see if anything looked odd to us. "If the killer had her keys . . ."

We nodded in understanding and followed him out our back door and into the back entrance to Dolly's apartment.

Warner Pier has an old-fashioned downtown business area, with two-story redbrick buildings. The show windows tend to be smaller than more modern ones, and the city fathers strongly encourage that all trim be white. The result is a town that looks as if Norman Rockwell painted it.

But few of our businesses really need their second stories, so most of them have converted the upstairs spaces into apartments. Some of the store owners live over their shops, but usually these are rented to seasonal employees. Housing is at a premium during the summer season, although lots of the apartments are empty during the winter. Some of them are not even heated well enough to occupy during the winter.

For several years before Dolly Jolly appeared in Warner Pier, Aunt Nettie hadn't bothered to rent out the apartment over TenHuis Chocolade. Handling the tenants was simply more trouble than the money was worth, she said, since they tended to be college kids who liked to party, annoyed the neighbors, weren't careful housekeepers, and who were casual about paying their rent.

But Dolly looked like a solid citizen, and she wanted to learn the chocolate business, so Aunt Nettie had had the apartment painted, had put up new window blinds, and had replaced the bathroom fixtures and the kitchen appliances. Dolly had a nice, solid apartment with a living room, eat-in kitchen, two bedrooms, bathroom, and a big closet that held a washer and dryer. There was an entrance from the alley and one from the street. If it had a problem, it was lack of light. The windows overlooking Fifth Street got a reasonable amount of sun, but the ones on the alley got almost none.

Dolly had her own furniture. She had inherited some antiques—nothing valuable, she said—and she had added a couch covered with mauve and burgundy flowers, a collection of old-fashioned cookware, and some nice floral prints. Dolly was a big woman. Somehow it was surprising to see how feminine her decorating taste was.

I hadn't been in Dolly's apartment often, but it looked normal to me. The bed was made, the dishes were done, the magazines— Dolly subscribed to all the *Gourmet*-type publications—were stacked neatly on the coffee table. I knew Dolly had carried the kitchen trash out before she left; I'd seen her do it when I came by to pick her up for the trip to the airport.

"It looks okay to me," I said. "Did the crime lab guys come up here?"

"Not yet. There may be no reason for them to come."

"I guess it would be a good place to hide," Aunt Nettie said. "At least for a few hours."

I shook my head. "Once we're all at work, you'd have to sit really still. We can hear people walking around up here, hear water running, stuff like that."

"This is such a small town," Aunt Nettie said. "It would be really hard to hide out in Warner Pier at all. You couldn't show a light, for example."

"Oh, Dolly left a lamp on one of those timers," I said. "She checked it before we left. It was set to come on at five o'clock and go off at midnight. And the lights in the back of the apartment couldn't be seen from the street. A person hiding up here could use the bathroom and kitchen after we'd all gone home."

I walked back to check the bathroom out. It looked fine. Dolly's towels were hanging straight on the towel racks. The counter held nothing but a large bottle of cologne, a can of hair spray, and cotton balls in a china dish.

I peeked into the big closet, the one that housed the washer and dryer. All Dolly's clothes hung neatly on their hangers. The dirty clothes hamper was closed. The lid of the washer was down. I peeked inside. Empty. For good measure, I checked the dryer. It held three or four towels.

The one in front was badly stained. I pulled it out. It was smeared with something red. The stain was a purplish red, and it wasn't a small stain.

"I wonder what this is?" I said.

Aunt Nettie looked over my shoulder. "It isn't blood," she said. "It's the wrong color."

Hogan gave a grunt. "You're an expert on bloodstains?"

"I've seen plenty of them," Aunt Nettie said. "Phil was on blood thinner the last five years of his life. I rinsed bloodstains out of his sheets and pajamas every week."

The proverbial lightbulb went off over my head. I turned to Hogan. "I suppose you went through the trash."

"There wasn't any trash up here."

"You might check the containers in the area."

"What for?"

"A box that held hair dye." I held the towel up. "I think someone dyed her hair up here."

Chapter 15

"And I think that person dyed her hair red," I said.

"Wait a minute," Hogan said. "Dolly is a redhead. Couldn't she have used this towel?"

"No. Dolly's hair is natural. She does not color it."

Aunt Nettie and I nodded like bobbleheads. We were both sure that Dolly's vivid hair was her natural color. After a moment of thought, I came up with the name of the guy who cut Dolly's hair.

"Ask him. He'll know," Aunt Nettie said. "He also ought to know if these stains are hair dye."

We left and went back to the shop. I assured Hogan I'd keep trying to reach Dolly. But when I called her cell phone, she still wasn't answering.

I also tried again to reach Joe. No luck there either. Until I ran through the calls on my answering machine, and there he was. He had called while we were upstairs in Dolly's apartment.

I growled at the sound of his voice. I wanted to talk to him. Not that he could do anything about the current crisis. I just needed to talk to him.

I listened to his message. "I heard you and Nettie have

more problems. I'm sorry I can't get over there now. I'll try to come by later."

He didn't tell me where he was or why he wasn't answering his cell phone.

What a day. I had confessed to interfering with a murder investigation, had confronted a Detroit mobster, had discovered a body, and had misplaced my husband. And it wasn't even time for lunch.

Lieutenant Underwood called the hairnet ladies together and asked if any of them had noticed any unusual activity in the alley or near the garage or around the doors to Dolly's apartment. No one said she had. Then Aunt Nettie sent them home. None of us was getting any work done, so there was little point in keeping them there. We all promised to be back bright and early the next day and to concentrate on turning the work out.

I nearly left myself, but I decided that the State Police would probably track me down and ask more questions. Besides, I was waiting for Dolly to call, and I'd left the office number. So, unfortunately, I didn't go home. Or maybe it was fortunately.

For lunch Aunt Nettie and I made ourselves peanut butter sandwiches from the stock of snacks in the break room. The press kept banging on the front door, and the lab crew was stomping around upstairs. The day was not improving.

After we'd eaten, Aunt Nettie decided to run the gauntlet of press and go home. She put her head down, went out the front door, and ran for her car. She jumped in and locked all the doors. Then she looked back at me, standing in the door, and we both began to laugh. The reporters had left, so she'd done her escape act with no audience.

She drove off, and I went back to my desk. When I sat down, I saw the telephone bill lying on top of a pile of papers, and I again wondered about the two phone numbers that had mystified me the night before. I'd told Hogan and Lieutenant Underwood about them, but I was still curious. So I picked up the phone on my desk and told it to block my outgoing calls from caller ID. Then I punched in the Atlanta number.

As I expected, it was answered by a woman's voice saying, "PDQ Investigations. How may I help you?"

I muttered about a wrong number and hung up. At least my suspicions had been confirmed.

Then I stared at the second number, the Chicago one, the line that had been answered by the man who called me names. I knew I ought to stay away from it, but I sure was curious.

I yielded to temptation and punched in that number.

After three rings, the guy with the raspy voice answered. "Yes."

"Hello. I'm calling from Warner Pier, Michigan, and I'm trying . . ."

Too late. "I told you not to call me anymore! Call Elliot! Is that plain enough? I don't want to talk to you."

Slam. End of call. I hadn't even been able to use my wrong number excuse.

Hmm. Maybe the State Police would tell me who was at that number—once they got around to requesting the information. I didn't think the unknown number—which might have no connection with Pamela—was a high priority in the investigation. But someday I'd like to finish reconciling the phone bill.

Meanwhile, I cleared the calls my answering machine had piled up since the last time I had checked. The *Grand Rapids*

Press. I killed the message. Moselle French, the nearest thing Warner Pier has to a grande dame. I didn't want to talk to her; message killed. George Jenkins, the other Warner Pier connection to the underground railroad. He wanted to know if he could help. He couldn't. Message killed. Then there were two actual business calls—retailers who order our chocolates. I wrote their numbers down so I could call them back, then killed their messages.

Next the answering machine played back a familiar voice. It was Webb Bartlett, a friend of Joe's who has a law practice in Grand Rapids. "Hi, Lee. I heard about the killing on the radio, so I know you're swamped. But I really need to find Joe. I've tried his cell, the shop, and your house. If you talk to him, tell him it's important that he talk to me. There have been developments since we talked at breakfast."

Webb? Webb was the person Joe had met for breakfast?

But why hadn't Joe told me that? He and I got together with Webb and his wife now and then. Why had Joe said he had to meet "a guy" instead of saying, "I'm getting together with Webb for breakfast."

Of course, then I might have asked why he and Webb were having a stag breakfast, rather than bringing their wives along for a nice dinner out.

Was Webb part of Joe's secret? Part of whatever had made Joe so uncommunicative lately?

I found Webb's card in my Rolodex, and my fingers caressed the telephone. But I laid the receiver down without calling. I didn't know where Joe was, so I had nothing to tell Webb, and I was determined not to interfere with Joe's problem—whatever the heck it was.

There was one more message on the answering machine—a

very meek Sarajane asked Aunt Nettie to call. I called her back, just to tell her to try Aunt Nettie at home.

She still sounded meek when she answered. "Peach Street B&B."

"Sarajane, I . . ."

Before I could say more, Sarajane gave a loud gasp. "You! Where are you?"

"I'm here at the office, Sarajane. Where you called. Is something wrong?"

Slight pause, then, "Who is this?"

"It's Lee, Sarajane."

"Oh!"

"Who did you think I was?"

"You sounded like Pamela."

"Pamela? But she's from Michigan. Have I lost my Texas drawl?"

"No. No, you haven't. I guess I just have Pamela on the brain. I'm even hearing her voice when she's not there."

Sarajane then launched into a big apology, begging us to forgive her for dragging us into Pamela's problems. I assured her that we didn't blame her.

"You didn't do it on purpose, Sarajane."

"I still feel guilty. And now Myrl's dead."

"You certainly can't blame yourself for that. Myrl brought Pamela to you, remember? You didn't introduce Pamela to her. I just called to tell you Aunt Nettie has gone home. I don't know if she's answering her phone, but you can try her there."

We left it at that.

The day dragged on. Hogan called to confirm that Dolly's hairstylist said she didn't color her hair. The hair stylist also thought the stains on the towels we'd found in the dryer were red dye.

"We'll turn the lab loose on it," Hogan said. "But it sounds as if you and Nettie were right."

I hung up and tried to picture Pamela as a killer. She was certainly the person who had the best opportunity to shoot Myrl, hide her body in Dolly's garage, and use her apartment to dye her hair. Or was she the killer's second victim? Had some other person done all those things? After all, we were sure Pamela could not have killed Derrick Valentine. She had a solid alibi from Sarajane and—indirectly—Rhett Spivey for that death.

I was deep in concentration on Pamela when the phone rang again. Maybe I only imagined it, but the ring sounded urgent. And when I looked at the caller ID, it was Dolly.

Finally.

I snatched the phone off the hook and spoke before she even had a chance to say hello. "I have so much to tell you that it's hard to start. But you don't color your hair, do you?"

"Color my hair!" Dolly gave her loud, ho-ho-ho laugh. "If I did, I'd ask for a more normal-looking color than the one I have. But what's going on up there? Is everybody all right?"

"Yes. I mean, no. Dolly, things are complicated here. Sit down."

I started with the death of Derrick Valentine and finished up with Dolly's Jeep being missing and her apartment being invaded. I tried to keep it short.

"I'm so sorry, Dolly! We just don't understand what's happened up here. It looks as if the killer stole your car. We can hope that it will not be harmed."

"Gosh, Lee!" I held the phone away from my ear. Dolly

always talks at top volume. Her whisper is what the rest of us call a shout. "I can't take all this in."

"I don't blame you. I'm just sorry about the car."

"I don't care about that Jeep! Somebody's dead?"

"Two people are dead, Dolly. But I don't think they're people who have anything to do with you."

"Still . . . You and Nettie have had a heck of a time. And you say Pamela is missing?"

"Yes, only she's not really Pamela Thompson. She's Christina Meachum. I mean, Belcher."

"You're not making sense!" Dolly was still shouting.

I had to backtrack and explain further. Our conversation got more detailed. But I finally staggered through the whole story.

"Now let me get this straight!" Dolly screamed. "This Pamela Thompson is really the ex-wife of that Detroit crook, Harold Belcher—Belcher the Butcher."

"That's right."

There was a long silence. "You know, that can't be right," Dolly said. This time her voice was only slightly loud.

"Why not?"

"Because I remember the Belcher case especially because Mrs. Belcher grew up in Ann Arbor. And that's where I grew up."

"I know. Did you go to school with her?"

"Nope. But I know Ann Arbor. And Pamela didn't."

"What do you mean?"

"I mean that someone asked Pamela where she was from, one day at lunch, and she said, Ann Arbor, so I tried the old hometown bit on her. You know, where'd you go to high school? Who was your English teacher? Like that."

"So?"

"So she didn't know anything about Ann Arbor. She'd never heard of the Fleetwood Diner. She couldn't tell me which high school she went to. She ate Oscar Mayer hot dogs without complaining, instead of holding out for Kowalski's Kwality with the natural casing. Nobody from eastern Michigan does that. I mean, they may eat some other hot dog, but they don't look blank when you mention Kowalski's Kwality."

Dolly paused again. "When Pamela saw that she'd goofed, she told me she'd only lived in Ann Arbor a year. But I didn't think she'd ever even been in the town. I always thought there was something funny about her."

I urged her to call Hogan immediately. He needed to know about that. In fact, he needed to know several things Dolly could tell him.

Dolly and I had talked nearly half an hour before we hung up. She wasn't going to have a minute left on her cell phone plan.

I gave a deep sigh and stared at my computer screen. I'd learned at least one amazing thing from Dolly.

She didn't think the woman we'd known as Pamela had ever lived in Ann Arbor. But Christina Meachum Belcher had supposedly grown up there.

I pulled out my file folder and looked at the pictures I'd taken off the Internet. I laid the pictures of Harold Belcher aside and stared at the ones of Christina.

Such a pretty girl. Big brown eyes. Beautiful heart-shaped face with a deep widow's peak, wide cheekbones, and a pointed chin. Dark hair piled up on top of her head.

I tried to picture her with the bleached blond hair Pamela

had had. Pamela had had bangs, long bangs that hid much of her face. And her jaw had been misshapen from the beating she's taken.

I connected with the Internet and Googled "Christina Meachum Belcher."

If Pamela wasn't from Ann Arbor, why was she claiming that she was?

Chapter 16

People always talk as if finding something on the Internet is—well, automatic. You type in your subject, and the information magically appears on your screen.

Reality, of course, is different. Unless the information has been posted on some site that can be accessed from the Internet, you're not going to find it at all. If it has been posted, it may be listed along with a thousand or more other sites. It can take hours to wade through them to find the one that contains the information you're looking for. If any of them do.

That was the situation for information on Christina Meachum Belcher.

Christina wasn't a famous person. She was simply a woman whose husband got in a lot of trouble. The Detroit newspapers had a lot about Harold the Butcher, but hardly anything about the prime witness against him, housewife Christina Meachum Belcher. And what I found was duplicated over and over. News writers are apparently too lazy to create entirely new stories. Once I read the phrase "whom sociologists have called a classic battered wife," I knew I was reading an excerpt from the same darn article all over again. Not only did news writers plagiarize from one another—they plagiarized from themselves. One particular writer called Christina "a battered wife who—fearing death—finally rebelled" in no fewer than ten articles. I decided he had kept the phrase stored in his computer and automatically plugged it in early in every story he wrote.

Few of these articles had been accompanied by pictures of Christina. And if they did have pictures, often they weren't displayed online. In the latest articles—the stories about Harold's most recent trial—Christina had been photographed while heavily disguised.

But an hour into the search, when I was down to the 132nd online reference to Christina, I got some actual information. A biography of Christina had run as a sidebar—I think that's what newspaper people call an extra background article—for a *Detroit Free Press* story about Harold's first trial.

"Her high school friends in Ann Arbor remember a sweet, dark-haired girl who made good grades in English and competed in speech tournaments, but who didn't have a lot of self-confidence," it read.

Hmmm. Ann Arbor again. Journalists were sure Christina had been reared in Ann Arbor, but Dolly was just as sure that she hadn't been. Did it matter?

Maybe not, I admitted to myself. But I was still curious, so I kept reading.

" 'Christy never felt sure of herself,' said Jack Vecchio, who escorted the young woman to their senior prom. 'Her mom made her take part in speech competitions, or so Christy told me, because she thought it would help her become more poised.' "

I felt a pang of sympathy for Pamela or Christy or whoever she was. My mom had pushed me into scholarship pageants, the kind that feed into the Miss Texas competition, because she thought it would help me develop poise. Most of the other contestants had seemed to enjoy the pageants, but the main thing I got out of the experience was learning how to smile when I was publicly branded a loser. That and a first husband who wanted to show off his beauty queen wife as long as she kept her mouth shut. I guess I did learn how to fake poise. I certainly never felt it.

The article went on along predictable lines, but then I noticed an item at the top of the computer page. There were three photo captions for pictures of Christy Meachum Belcher. These, I gathered, were different photographs from the one I'd found earlier, the picture taken at a fancy party. But the photos were not on that Web page.

Maybe that was what made me wild to see them. How could I get a look at those photos?

I called the Warner Pier Public Library and asked if they had the *Detroit Free Press* on microfilm. Microfilm, I learned, was now a thing of the past.

"If you want to look at a *Detroit Free Press* published since the year 2000," the reference librarian said, "you can use a database."

"Is there a fee?"

"Not if you have a library card. The Michigan Department of Libraries pays for all state libraries to use that database."

"I'll be right over."

"Come ahead. Unless you want to access it from your own computer."

"I can do that?"

"Certainly." The librarian explained how, and she didn't even sound condescending. Librarians are wonderful people.

In less than five minutes, I was looking at the article about Christina Meachum. There were the pictures I'd wanted to see. Christina's high school graduation picture. Of course, it looked nothing like Pamela. All of us change in twenty years. Next was a photo from a mob wedding—a different picture from the one I'd seen earlier, but apparently the same event. And then there was Christina's own wedding picture.

And no matter how I tried, I could not turn the bride in that picture into Pamela Thompson. It was more than the nearly twenty-year age difference. It simply didn't look like the same person.

This was confusing. After all, when I'd seen the ID-type picture Derrick Valentine had displayed, I had immediately thought it was Pamela. I tried to analyze why I couldn't picture Pamela as the young girl in the lacy wedding gown.

The first thing was the eye makeup. As a young bride, Christina had worn hardly any eye makeup. Maybe some mascara. By the time the ID photo was taken she was circling her eyes with dark liner, sculpting the brow line with eye shadow, and loading the mascara on with a trowel. As Pamela, she still wore that eye makeup.

Pamela's face was now a different shape, as well. Today her jaw was misshapen—what my Texas grandmother would have called "whopperjawed." It was lumpy on one side. I had assumed Harold "the Butcher" Belcher had arranged that change.

Pamela's hair was different from her days as Christina as well. It was more than the color—which had changed from Christina's lustrously dark hair to Pamela's cheap-looking blond. The style was also completely different. Pamela had used heavy bangs and a long bob to cover up as much of her face as possible. Christina had pulled her hair back, showing her deep widow's peak and dainty ears.

I pictured one of the last times I had talked to Pamela face-to-face, on the afternoon Derrick Valentine had been looking for her. She had been sitting at the table in the break room, making bows in Easter colors. I had told her the picture Valentine had shown me was definitely her, and her reaction had been odd.

Pamela had smirked.

When she saw my reaction—the smirk had astonished me, and I'm sure I showed it—Pamela had dropped her face into her hands, pushing her bangs back from her forehead.

I gasped as I remembered. Pamela had a broad, high forehead.

Next Pamela had pulled her hairnet off, then put it back on, tucking the long side hair into it, and keeping the brashly blond stuff pulled down to cover her ears.

But I'd gotten a glimpse of them. They weren't pretty ears. They were large, with pendulant lobes. I remembered thinking that Pamela needed always to wear her hair in a style that covered them.

Now I looked at Christina's wedding picture again. Her ears were small, and the dainty lobes were adorned with tiny pearl drops.

And her forehead wasn't broad and square. She had that deep widow's peak.

I didn't gasp again. But I was sure. Whoever the underground railroad had been helping to escape, whoever the woman was that we'd known as Pamela, she had not been Christina Meachum Belcher.

I stared at the photo, taking in my new idea. Pamela was not Christina? But Myrl and her underground railroad cohorts had said she was. Sarajane believed it. How could it not be true?

It was simply too fantastic to believe.

I had figured it out, true, and I probably should have called Hogan immediately. But I had to take it in emotionally before I could start spreading the word.

At the time all I felt was a deep longing to talk to Joe. Joe thought logically. Maybe if I explained it to him, he would see the flaw in my reasoning. Maybe once again Pamela would morph into Christina, and I wouldn't feel as if the world had turned upside down.

I tried his shop, his cell phone, the Warner Pier City Hall, and our house. I even called his mom. But she said she hadn't heard from him.

"Have you been leaving messages for Joe?" I asked.

"I left one at your house. And, yes, I left one at the shop. And one on his cell phone."

"I wonder where he could be? He doesn't usually get completely out of touch."

We agreed that his behavior was odd, but neither of us was worried. Then I called Webb Bartlett, to find out if Joe had checked in with him.

Webb said that he hadn't heard from Joe. "I really need to talk to him," he said. "Has he ever explained this whole idea to you?"

"No, Webb. I didn't even know he'd been talking to you."

"Well, I'd better let Joe tell it." Then he seemed to realize how I might interpret that. "It's nothing bad, Lee! Just a little deal he and I have been talking about."

"Deal?"

"A job I'm trying to get him to take on."

Oh. As an attorney with a busy practice, Webb always had lots of minor odd jobs he needed help with. He'd asked Joe for help before, but Joe had always declined. I put the whole thing out of my mind. I sent greetings to Webb's wife, and we promised to get together soon. Then I hung up.

I hadn't forgotten Pamela, even if I couldn't talk to Joe about her.

Apparently Pamela—whoever she really was—had convinced the abused women's rescue group that she was Christina Meachum and was badly in need of help escaping her dangerous ex-husband. But if Pamela wasn't Christina, why had Harold Belcher shown up in Warner Pier, demanding that Aunt Nettie and I tell him where she was?

And where was the real Christina?

I stared at the wall. My discoveries were beginning to sink in. I knew I had to find Hogan and tell him that I didn't think our Pamela was Christina Meachum Belcher.

I took my time doing it. I put on my ski jacket, boots, and hat. I went out of the shop and locked the door behind myself. I walked slowly down the street and over a block to City Hall. I sauntered around the building and into the police department, steeling myself to talk to Hogan.

He wasn't there.

The office was empty except for the secretary-dispatcher, a woman named Judy VanRynn. "You just missed them," she said. "Hogan and Lieutenant Underwood left about ten minutes ago. They went over to the Lake Michigan Inn to quiz that O'Sullivan guy."

For a moment I couldn't remember who in the world O'Sullivan was. I guess I looked as blank as I felt, because Judy explained.

"That other Atlanta private eye."

"O'Sullivan! Oh! Did he come back to Warner Pier?"

"Yah." Judy answered with that western Michigan version of "yeah" that sounds almost like the "Ja" of the original Dutch settlers. She picked up a pink message pad. "Can I tell Hogan what you need?"

"Yes. It's a message for either Hogan or Lieutenant Underwood."

"Okay."

I knelt beside her desk and lowered my voice, almost to a whisper, even though only the two of us were in the office. "Tell them I don't think Pamela is Christina."

Now it was Judy's turn to look blank. "You don't think Pamela is Christina? What the heck does that mean?"

She spoke without lowering her voice. The words just bounced around all over the police department, followed by a giant silence as I tried to think how to explain.

But the silence didn't last. It was broken by a huge roar.

"Not Christina? Then where the hell is my wife?"

Chocolate Chat
Making Chocolate Chocolate

From bean to bar, producing chocolate for eating is a complicated process.

Fat—cocoa butter—is removed to make it a dry powder. It may be treated with alkalines, or "Dutched." This powder is the basis of cocoa.

Fat is then returned to the cocoa, and sugar is added, as well as other flavorings, such as vanilla. For milk chocolate, of course, milk is added—either powdered, condensed, or in small clumps.

The resulting mass is then "conched." This is a grinding and mixing process that may go on for days and produces the velvety texture of good chocolate. The earliest conching machines used grinding stones shaped like conch shells.

"Tempering" is a process used to keep chocolate from developing "bloom." Bloom is those white spots found on chocolate that has become too warm or too damp. It doesn't hurt the chocolate for eating, but is not considered attractive.

Happily, chocolate that gets "out of temper" can be melted and tempered again.

Chapter 17

Harold Belcher was coming out of the hall that led to the men's room, and he seemed to be in attack mode.

He roared again. "What do you mean, Pamela isn't Christina?"

"I don't know!" I blurted out the words, so scared that I nearly left a puddle on the floor. "Everybody said she was Christina, but I looked at her pictures, and I can't see it!"

He glared at me. I fought the impulse to hide under Judy's desk and forced myself to glare back. Then I heard my voice again. "What are *you* doing here, anyway?"

Judy had jumped to her feet and was making some effort at controlling her office. "Just calm down!"

Harold ignored her and answered my question. "I came in to talk to your blankety-blank police chief! Everybody kept telling me to check with the authorities, so I thought I'd do it. Now you say you've lost Christina!"

"I never had Christina!" That was me.

"Calm down! Everybody stop yelling!" That was Judy.

"Where the hell is my wife?"

"Ex-wife!"

"Calm down!"

Either Judy prevailed, or Harold and I ran out of things to yell at each other. Anyway, Harold didn't seem to have a meat cleaver or any other weapon, and his fists were not balled into clubs. I threw myself down in one of the visitor's chairs. "Judy, you'd better get Hogan over here pinto! I mean, pronto! I'll wait for him!"

Harold growled and sat down in a chair that faced mine. We both folded our arms and glared at each other.

"Yeah," Harold said. "Get the chief over here. And that state cop. Let's figure this out."

Judy punched buttons on the radio. "Hogan, you better come back to the office," she said. "I've got a minor riot going on over here. Harold Belcher came in, and he was waiting to see you. Then Lee Woodyard showed up, and she says she has some new information. They're not getting along."

There was a pause. Then Judy broke off the radio connection. "Hogan and Lieutenant Underwood will be here right away. You two just sit there and stay calm."

"I'm not going anywhere," I said. The truth was that I felt fairly safe inside the police department—even with no uniformed officers present. It didn't seem likely that Harold Belcher would go into his butcher act right in the police station. I had no idea what he would do if I left and he followed me outside, and I didn't want to find out. I probably wasn't thinking rationally. But I stayed put.

Judy must have convinced Hogan of the seriousness of the situation, because he and Lieutenant Underwood were there within five minutes. Then real calm prevailed, replacing the armed camp that the police department office had been for Harold Belcher, Judy, and me.

First, Hogan and Underwood took me into Hogan's office,

and closed the door firmly, leaving Harold in the outer office. I explained my research and the reasons why I had concluded that the "Pamela" Aunt Nettie and I had given sanctuary was not Christina Belcher—even though Sarajane and Myrl had believed that she was.

Hogan asked the first question. "Did this woman—let's keep calling her Pamela—ever tell you she was Christina Meachum Belcher?"

"No. I never learned who she was supposed to be until after she had left. Aunt Nettie and Sarajane just told me that she was in desperate danger from her ex-husband. When I learned she was supposed to be Christina Belcher, I could see why they thought so."

"But you don't think she looks like the pictures of Christina Belcher?"

"At first I did. Remember that I was told that she'd been brutally beaten. The pictures I found of Christina were taken before her injuries, so I didn't expect her to look exactly like them. Pamela's face is misshapen, for example. And she had dyed her hair. But the eyes have a real close resemblance. At first I felt sure it *was* the same person. It's only within the past half hour that I realized that Pamela's ears and hairline were different from Christina's."

Hogan looked at Underwood. "Then who is this Pamela? Besides being the main suspect in at least one murder."

Neither of them had an answer. They told me I could go. But as I got up, Hogan spoke. "Pamela spent the night at your house?"

"Yes."

"Have you cleaned the room yet?"

"I stripped the bed and washed the sheets, but I haven't swept. And I haven't touched the bathroom she used."

"Don't. Leave everything. We may want to send the crime scene crew out there."

"I guess you might find fingerprints. Or a hair or something you could use to check the DNA."

Underwood sighed. "I hope we figure it out sooner than that."

Hogan had told me the state lab was backed up for months with DNA checks. So I nodded and left, being careful not to look at Harold Belcher as I went out the door.

I hadn't walked more than half a block when I realized that I had not told Hogan and Underwood about one thing. When they asked if I had cleaned Pamela's room, I forgot to mention finding the class ring, the man's class ring on a chain. The one marked FSC, with a fierce cat of some sort silhouetted on the blue stone.

I immediately turned around and went back to add that information. But I was too late. The two of them were closeted with Harold Belcher. Judy wasn't willing to call Hogan on the phone, and I certainly wasn't willing to knock on the door. So I wrote a note about the ring, and I left it with Judy. Then I went back to the office, feeling that I'd done all I could.

But, naturally, I was still curious. So I got out my *New York Times World Almanac* and looked at the "Colleges and Universities" list. While there were state universities listed beginning with F—Florida State, for example, and Fort Hays State in Kansas—there were only three "state colleges" that began with that letter. Farwell State College, Farwell, Oklahoma; Fitchburg State College, Fitchburg, Massachusetts; and Framingham State College, Framingham, Massachusetts.

Hmm. Pamela pronounced her R's, so I didn't see her as having a New England background. I checked the Internet for Farwell State in Farwell, Oklahoma. Naturally the school had a Web site.

Farwell State had been founded more than a hundred years ago as a teachers' college, the Web site said. That left me unsurprised. I knew the colleges in western states—like Oklahoma and my old home, Texas—had been established for that reason. The churches had established colleges to train ministers, and the states had set up colleges to train teachers. Other professions and fields of knowledge had come later.

The Farwell State mascot was the Cougar, and its colors were gold and blue. That went along with the color and mascot on the class ring. The college Web site had plenty of "Cougar Spirit." It bragged about the college's accomplishments. It didn't just list athletic successes, either. There was a whole section on academic honors, and another on alumni who had made it big.

I could tell the Web site hadn't been updated recently. The athletic section was over a year old. The actress they listed as nominated for an Academy Award had since won, but that news wasn't there. Farwell State needed to hire a new webmaster.

But the mascot and the color of the stone in the class ring made me willing to bet that whoever the woman we knew as Pamela was, she had had some connection to the Oklahoma college.

I was curious enough that I looked through the list of prominent alumni in more detail. And there, under the "Business" category, I found an interesting name.

"Patricia Youngman." She had graduated exactly twenty years earlier. For a moment I couldn't place the name, though it sounded familiar. Then I read the description of her job.

"Chief of Staff to Marson Endicott, CEO of the Prodigal Corporation."

"Golly!" I breathed the word.

Patricia Youngman—the woman Potty Mouth had cursed on the television. The woman who had fled the country with the Prodigal Corporation records. The woman both Marson Endicott and—supposedly—federal investigators were trying to find.

But Patricia Youngman couldn't be in Warner Pier, Michigan. She was in Africa, in some country that had no extradition treating with the United States. I'd seen her on CNN.

Hadn't I?

I pictured the woman I'd seen on the news report. She had a blond pageboy, a floppy hat, and big sunglasses. Heck, she could have been anybody.

Could Pamela be Patricia Youngman?

Nah.

But I decided to check. I Googled her name and pulled up ten thousand-plus references to the famous fugitive.

And the very first one showed a good clear picture of a woman with a broad, square forehead.

It didn't seem possible. But that forehead was like the one Pamela had kept carefully covered by heavy bangs until she forgot and pushed her hair back.

This time I didn't hesitate. I reached for the phone and called Hogan.

He still wasn't available, and Judy VanRynn was getting tired of taking messages from me. He and Lieutenant Underwood had, she said, disposed of Harold Belcher and gone back to the Lake Michigan Inn to deal with O'Sullivan.

What the heck, I decided, I'd go to the motel and try to find him. I put on coat, scarf, and hat, then headed out.

The Lake Michigan Inn is the lodging place most lacking in character of any lodging place in Warner Pier. We have quaint Victorian bed-and-breakfast inns out the kazoo, we have two old motels that have been remodeled into suites, we have a 1920s-era hotel that's been seriously renovated, but the Lake Michigan Inn is the only ordinary, plain vanilla motel in town.

Its owner lives there, so I guess it's cheap to operate. I mean, he's not turning the utilities off for the winter, so he keeps it open all year.

As I drove into the parking lot, it was almost empty. There were no law enforcement cars, either Warner Pier PD or Michigan State Police. There were only two private cars. One was a nondescript sedan with an Illinois license plate—the one I'd speculated belonged to the two guys in city overcoats I'd seen in Hogan's office. The second was a tan sedan with a Georgia license plate. That would belong to O'Sullivan. I didn't want to talk to him.

O'Sullivan was parked in the slot where I'd seen Rhett-the-butler's Cadillac Escalade the previous evening. The memory made me smile, and once again I wondered if Rhett had found local companionship, or if he had imported a girlfriend. Or maybe a guy friend. With a man who sometimes wore a pinkie ring, I wouldn't want to guess.

I paused in the parking lot and considered Rhett's pinkie ring. It had had a blue stone with some sort of black design imposed on it. Had it been a class ring?

Surely it couldn't have been a ring matching the one Pamela had lost in our spare bedroom.

Ridiculous.

But Farwell State College could tell us. The college was sure to have an alumni relations office, and if it was anything like my alma mater—the University of Texas Dallas—they never lost track of an alumnus, at least not of one who had a paying job. They might not tell a plain old citizen like me where those alumni were, but they'd tell a detective. It wasn't privileged information. It had probably been printed in the FSC alumni magazine.

My heart began to pound as I remembered something else. Rhett had known Patricia Youngman. When Joe asked him about her, he answered, "She hired me."

And Patricia Youngman had a broad, square forehead like Pamela's.

"They're going steady?" I spoke aloud. Of course the idea was silly. High school kids exchanged class rings, not fortyish adults.

But still . . .

I decided it was time for me to hand my speculations over to Hogan and Lieutenant Underwood. And I'd hand the class ring over at the same time. I put the van in drive and headed for the house, where that ring ought to be in a pottery catchall vase on the mantelpiece.

As I drove the two miles to the house, I felt smug. I'd made some deductions that sounded good to me, and now, virtuously, I was going to turn them over to the proper authorities.

The main thing that bothered me was Joe's whereabouts. It was simply strange for him to disappear without a word to anyone. So I was greatly relieved when I saw his truck sitting in the driveway.

I jumped out of the van and rushed into the house, calling out his name. "Joe! Joe, where have you been? I was beginning to get worried."

I heard a movement in the living room, so I hurried toward the sound. "Joe? I talked to Webb, he's been trying to find you. So has your mom. Where were you?"

I tried to come to a stop as I went through the dining room, but I stumbled over my heavy boots, and I nearly went flying. I caught myself on the door frame and stopped, astonished by the figure standing by the fireplace.

It wasn't Joe. It was a redheaded woman holding a pistol. She had it pointed at me.

Chapter 18

The broad forehead told me who she was.

I was facing Patricia Youngman, one of the most-wanted fugitives in the world, and she had a gun.

She certainly looked different from the way she had when disguised as Pamela. Her eye makeup was tasteful and restrained, and her face was symmetrical. Her eyes were blue instead of brown.

But Patricia couldn't possibly be aware that I had figured out who she was. I hoped she didn't even know that Myrl's body had been found.

Was I clever enough to hide my knowledge of her identity? Or would hiding it *be* clever? Should I simply admit I recognized her?

And if so, who was she? Or who did she want me to think she was? Pamela? Christina? Patricia?

At least she hadn't shot me yet.

I eyed the pistol, took a deep breath, and jumped off the dock into deep water. "Pamela! Your hair! I like it short. And the color's great. But I thought you would be far, far away by now! What are you doing here?"

Pamela kept the pistol pointed at me. "I hadn't finished my business in Warner Pier."

"Your business?" I tried to look confused. Pamela's business had been a routine job at a chocolate company. "Oh. Well, if there's any way I can help you, let me know."

I looked vacantly around the room. "Where's Joe?"

"He went somewhere."

"Without his truck? I guess he hasn't gone far."

Pamela—I tried to make myself think of her as Pamela—smirked. It was the same expression she'd had three days earlier when I told her Derrick Valentine had showed me a picture of her.

That smirk infuriated me. She'd been laughing at me three days earlier—laughing because I'd been so sure the picture was of her, when in truth it was a picture of a completely different person. Now she was laughing at me because Joe wasn't there, and his truck was, and she thought I was so dumb I'd believe she hadn't done anything to him.

Where was Joe? Had she killed him the way she must have killed Myrl? The cold of fear overcame the heat of anger, but I did my best to keep my usual dumb expression. Maybe I should even play hostess.

"Can I make you a cup of coffee?"

"No."

We looked at each other. I don't think either of us knew what to say next.

Finally I spoke. "I'd feel better if you'd put that pistol down, Pamela. I know you're in danger, but I'm not going to hurt you."

I was surprised when Patricia—I mean, Pamela—did lower

the pistol, pointing it toward the floor. At least it wasn't aimed at me.

"Let's sit down," I said.

Joe and I had arranged our couch and an easy chair at right angles to each other, in front of the fireplace. I walked three steps and sat down in the easy chair, so stiff that I merely perched on the edge of the cushion. Pamela sat down at the opposite end of the couch. She was wearing tight jeans, and when she sat down, she took one of those dadgum tubes of M&Ms out of her pocket. It still annoyed me.

We stared at each other. I tried to think of what I would say if Patricia were really Pamela.

"Listen," I said, "Warner Pier may be a bad place for you right now. Harold Belcher is hanging around town."

That drew another smirk. "I'm not worried about Harold Belcher."

"Have you been in touch with Sarajane?"

"No."

"She's been concerned about you and Myrl." I looked around the room. How could I get her to put that gun away? Or how could I take it away from her? What could distract her?

My eye rested on the fireplace. "Great! Joe laid a fire. I'll touch a match to it."

I moved fast, dropping to my knees on the hearth rug. We had a wrought-iron fire screen, the kind that's separate from the fireplace, not the built-in sort. I moved it aside, pulled a match from the box of extra-long matches in the wood basket, and struck a light.

"My great-grandfather built this fireplace, Patricia," I said as I touched the flame to the kindling under the logs. "The family is proud of it. It draws great."

The kindling caught, and I put the big matchbox back in the wood basket. Then I grabbed either side of the fire screen and picked it up, trying to look as if I wanted to replace it in front of the fireplace.

Instead I swung it toward Pamela as hard as I could, and it hit her with a horrible, eardrum-splitting explosion.

At least that was my impression at that moment. I was astonished by the noise the fire screen had made. And I was even more astonished when it fell to the floor and I saw that it had a hole in it.

And Patricia was pointing her pistol at me again.

"You called me Patricia," she said coldly.

In another second I had sorted the whole thing out. My tangled tongue had tripped me up. I had called Patricia by her right name—not by her fake one, Pamela. That had alerted her, and she had raised the pistol again. Kneeling on the hearth rug with my back to her, I hadn't realized that. She had already aimed the pistol when I had picked up the fire screen and swung it at her.

I don't yet know if swinging the fire screen saved my life or made her fire. She may not have known herself. All I knew at that moment was that Patricia—forget Pamela—was shoving the fire screen into the floor with one hand, and in the other she held Sarajane's little silver automatic.

And she was pointing the pistol at me again. Her finger was on the trigger.

"Nice try," she said. She was still smirking. "I think I'd better put you away, Mrs. Woodyard."

I closed my eyes and thought of my Texas grandmother.

She had died when I was fifteen. Would I be seeing her in a moment? But Grandma wouldn't want me to die tamely. If Patricia was going to kill me anyway, I might as well go out fighting.

I tensed my muscles and opened my eyes. And that pistol was right in front of the left one. I was looking down the barrel.

I might still have tried to attack Patricia, but she spoke before I could move. "I'm not going to kill you, Lee! I just can't let you call the cops."

Now the pistol was touching my forehead.

"You'll be okay. You and your husband both. But don't try another stupid stunt!"

I didn't answer, but I didn't move. Joe. She had said Joe would be all right if I didn't act "stupid." Hope flickered.

"Okay," Patricia said. "I'm going to stand up. You're not going to move. Got it?"

I didn't respond, so she poked me with the gun. "Say yes!"

"Yes." My voice was a whisper. I was afraid to nod.

Patricia stood up, and she moved until the couch was between us. "Now you stand up. Slowly."

I obeyed.

"Good. Now, turn around."

"Can I put the fire screen up?"

Patricia gave a harsh laugh. "Sure. We don't want the house to burn down, do we?"

She backed up, farther out of my reach, and motioned with the pistol. I propped the fire screen in front of the fireplace. Joe built great fires. His kindling was crackling away, and I could see a log beginning to catch.

When I stood up, Patricia spoke. "Now, walk into the kitchen. Slowly."

The kitchen? That seemed odd, but I did it.

"Go out in that back hall. Don't do anything sudden. Just walk out there and face the basement door."

Our house is just over a hundred years old, and it has an architectural feature I never saw in Texas. It's known as a Michigan basement.

A Michigan basement has walls of cement or stone, but the floor is sand. It's been dug deep enough that the floor lies below the freeze line, so it would have been ideal for storing potatoes, in the days when people bought the winter's supply of potatoes. It isn't much use as a game room and even requires remodeling if the homeowner wants to put a washing machine down there.

Our particular Michigan basement also features a large, heavy-duty bolt on the outside of the door.

I didn't understand why Patricia wanted me to face the basement door. But I obeyed. Then I saw that the bolt on the basement door had been thrown. The door was bolted shut.

She must have locked Joe in the basement.

Just as I realized that, Patricia yelled, right in my ear, "Woodyard! You'd better not be near that door!"

I heard another roar. And I screamed. A hole appeared in the lower half of the basement door.

Patricia had fired a bullet right through it. I could only hope Joe hadn't been in the line of fire.

"Now, Lee," she said. "Open the door."

I pushed the bolt back and pushed the door open.

The light from the hall fell down the stairs, and Joe lay at the bottom. He wasn't moving.

"Joe!" I didn't wait for Patricia to tell me to join him.

I clattered down the bare, wooden stairs. I think I only touched every other step. Joe was hurt. He was just lying there, injured. Had she shot him? Oh, God! Please don't let him be dead!

Just as I got to the bottom of the stairs, I heard the basement door slam, and the room became pitch-dark.

I had been in the process of falling to my knees. Now I had to stop, feel around, and make sure I wasn't jamming those knees into Joe's rib cage.

"Joe? Joe?"

Then a hand ran up my arm. I screamed. It tightened on my left bicep. A different hand covered my mouth.

"Quiet!" It was Joe's voice. "Hush up! I want her to think she's knocked me out."

I began to cry. Joe was trying to sit up, and I was trying to hug his neck, and neither of us could see the other, and we probably looked like snakes wrestling. But no one could have seen us, of course, because it was dark.

Joe finally decided I understood about keeping quiet, and took his hand off my mouth. I finally got a satisfactory grip on him. Talk about a clinch. I grabbed him so hard he could hardly breathe.

In a moment I whispered in his ear, "I was so frightened."

Joe whispered back, "How do you think I felt when I heard that gunshot?"

After that we just held each other for a few moments. Then Joe whispered again. "What say we turn on the light?"

We fumbled until I convinced Joe I should be the one to get to my feet and find the light switch. Our house may be old, but it does have a light switch at both the top and the bottom of the basement stairs.

When the bare bulb in the center of the basement went on, it looked as cheerful as a sunrise. Joe was getting to his feet, and his right pant leg had a bloodstain four or five inches across.

"Joe, you really are hurt!"

Joe shrugged. "I could use a Band-Aid. I don't think anything's broken, because I can move my leg easily. But my knee is swelling up like a watermelon. I don't suppose she tossed an ice pack down with you."

"How did she get you down here?" Then I realized what a stupid question that was. "Duh. I guess she used that gun."

"She made me put my hands on top of my head. Then when I got a couple of steps down, she kicked me right in the fanny." Joe rubbed the spot. "Not a very dignified way to get injured. I had to jump the rest of the way. I fell and landed on my knee."

"And you had the presence of mind to pretend to be seriously injured."

Joe nodded. "I don't know if it was presence of mind or terror. I was expecting her to start shooting. This is one time I don't like living in a secluded location."

I nodded. It was around four in the afternoon. We had few close neighbors, and the ones we did have would be at work. The chances of anyone hearing the gunshots were nil.

I wanted to look at Joe's injury, but he brushed my concerns aside. But he did move the leg carefully as he got up from the floor and sat down on one of the lower steps. "And now I've got a question for you," he said.

"What?"

"Just why the hell does the TenHuis family home have a bolt on the outside of the basement door? Are you afraid the mice are going to climb upstairs and raid the kitchen?"

The question struck me as funny. I put my hand over my own mouth and began to laugh. I may have rolled on the sandy floor. At least I know that I later discovered I had sand in my hair. Finally I was able to whisper an answer.

"It was Santa Claus's fault," I said. "And my mom's. She was much younger than Uncle Phil, you know. The story is that when she was about three my grandparents hid the Christmas presents in the basement, where she was forbidden to go. But she got down there and found them. Mom now swears Uncle Phil put her up to it. Anyway, my grandfather put a bolt on the door, up high where she couldn't reach it.

"Uncle Phil told me it took her less than twenty-four hours to figure how to push a chair over there and get in anyway. But she didn't let them catch her again. So you have your mother-in-law to thank for being locked in the Michigan basement."

"I probably have her to thank for being alive. If that woman—I assume she's Patricia Youngman—hadn't had a place to lock me in, she would probably have killed me."

"How did you know she's Patricia Youngman?"

"Oh, I have my sources. Now, let's figure a way out of here."

I looked around the basement. It was almost empty. After Aunt Nettie remarried and moved away, she and I had a giant clean-out of the whole house. The basement tended to collect insects and the mice Joe had referred to. A Michigan basement might be perfect for storing potatoes, but no one would store good wooden furniture down there. Or out-of-season clothes. Or the wedding china and extra blankets. Even plastic storage bins or trunks would be likely to be invaded by the tiny inhabitants.

The hot water heater stood on a slab of concrete in the back corner, and there was a similar slab of concrete at the foot of the stairs. That was probably what had injured Joe's knee. A brick column squarely in the middle of the space supported the fireplace. A set of rough wooden shelves in a corner held a few canning jars and what looked like a cleaning rag.

The only piece of furniture was an old iron bed frame, with white paint scaling off it. It was a recent addition to the basement. Joe had found it in the rafters of the garage when he took a notion to clean out there several months earlier. I'd put it in the pile of junk that we planned to take to the dump, but Aunt Nettie had said she saw one like it in an antique shop. All we'd have to do was sand and paint it, she said. Then we could sell it for—well, maybe as much as twenty-five dollars. Aunt Nettie had talked me into keeping it, and she and I had moved it to the darkest corner of the basement. It was still sitting there, unsanded and unpainted. And useless in the present emergency, as far as I could see.

I gestured toward the shelves. "I guess we could tear a couple of boards off those shelves and start tunneling. We ought to be able to dig under the wall in a couple of months."

"Yeah, and by then we'll be frozen so stiff we can use our fingers as picks."

For the first time I realized that Joe didn't have a jacket. I did. I hadn't taken mine off when I came in and confronted Patricia. I'd still been wearing it when she forced me into the basement. I started to pull it off. "We can share this jacket."

"Keep it," Joe said. "So far I'm okay." He was wearing a flannel shirt and flannel-lined jeans, and he usually wears long johns in the winter. I was afraid his knee had bled badly, since the blood had soaked through two layers before it got to the outside of his pants.

"I guess the crawl space under the bathroom won't work," I said.

"Nope. I bricked it in solidly."

The previous summer I had gotten out of the house by crawling under an addition to the bathroom—an addition that didn't have a basement itself, but was connected to the basement we were in by a hole in the wall left for the future convenience of plumbers. From there I had managed to get out through a hole in the foundation. But that addition had been under construction at the time. Now it was complete, and the foundation was solid.

Joe sighed. "I was hoping you'd reveal the existence of a secret tunnel known only to the TenHuis family. If that's out, I guess the windows are the best bet."

I looked at the windows. They were typical basement windows, small rectangles originally designed to be opened for ventilation. However, somebody among my TenHuis ancestors had decided to fix them in permanently. They could only be opened by an ax or a crowbar. Plus, at the moment they were covered with snow. There were two on the east and two on the west. Each was about a quarter the size of a regular window, and each had three panes.

"I wish the TenHuis family crowbar was stored down here," I said.

"Yeah. I've been working on one of the windows with my pocketknife, but I think digging under the wall would be faster." Joe stood up.

I looked around longingly. "How about the iron bed?"

"What iron bed?"

"The one over in the corner."

"I didn't see that. I guess it was behind the chimney. I doubt it has a sharp end."

Through all of this, of course, we were still whispering. Neither of us had forgotten that noise could mean death. Motioning for Joe to sit still and keep weight off his knee, I went to the bed frame. I picked up the smaller piece—the foot of the bed. Although it was the spindly kind of iron bed, made with small iron rods and knobs, it still weighed a lot. I dragged it back to where Joe sat.

He examined it. "Maybe . . ." The thing was rickety. Although it was rusty, Joe was able to twist it apart. He yanked off an iron leg, which proved to be a pipe about the length of a crowbar.

But when the leg came off, the larger piece began to fall. I barely caught it before it crashed into the cement wall. The noise could have been—well, maybe fatal.

I crouched on the sandy floor, clutching the bed frame and holding my breath. Joe didn't move either. We were listening for Patricia Youngman's footsteps.

And we heard them. Moving over our heads, crossing the living room floor.

"Quick!" Joe slid to the floor, taking the position he'd had when I ran down the stairs. I dragged the bed frame around under the stairs. Then I knelt beside Joe, prepared to weep, wail, and beg Patricia Youngman to call an ambulance.

I've never been as relieved in my life as I was at the next sound I heard from upstairs.

The television set came on.

Chapter 19

I leaned close to Joe's ear. "Sarajane said she was one of those people who always want the television set on."

"Good for her! It might help cover any noise we make."

We waited for a moment, listening for more footsteps, footsteps that would mean Patricia was walking into the kitchen and back hall, coming to check on us.

"We left the light on," I whispered.

"That's okay," he murmured back. "I'm the only one who's supposed to be unconscious. It would look fishy if you hadn't turned on the light."

Joe got up, protecting his knee. I could see that it was painful, but I didn't say any more about it. I didn't have an ice bag or a splint or even a Band-Aid, so there was no point in talking about it.

Joe hobbled over to the west wall, holding the pipe he'd wrenched from the bed frame. Now I saw that before I came down he'd been digging out the mortar at one of the windows. He picked up the pipe and examined just how it could be used.

"I wish the end were sharper," he said. "Maybe I can make a bigger hole with my knife, then use the pipe."

Luckily, Joe's pocketknife wasn't one of those wimpy little penknives. It was more on the Swiss Army Knife pattern, with two strong blades, a nail file that could tear a fingernail to shreds, and a corkscrew.

"I never needed this corkscrew before," Joe said.

"What do you need it for now?"

"I could use a drink. If we get out of here, my next project will be to put in some wine racks."

I chuckled appreciatively and quietly. If I was going to be imprisoned in a Michigan basement, it was good to have a fellow prisoner who tried to keep my spirits up.

Joe kept digging at the wood of the window frame. We could both see that it would take days to make any headway with only a pocketknife and a one-inch pipe. Plus the window frame was screwed to the foundation. Even with the piece of iron pipe from the bed frame, we weren't getting out of that window anytime soon. We couldn't tear the window out quietly. And if Patricia Youngman heard us, she'd be down that stairway in a second, spraying bullets in all directions.

In the meantime, Joe was standing on one leg, his head back at an awkward angle, working at a task that was higher than his head. He had to be in agony.

I moved close to him. "Can I take a turn?"

"Maybe later. Look around down here and see if you can find any other useful objects."

I blinked away a couple of tears. I knew Joe was merely giving me a job to keep me busy. We were at Patricia Youngman's mercy. I moved over to the old storage shelves, partly because turning away kept Joe from seeing that I was crying.

The shelves were nearly empty. Aunt Nettie and I had cleared out the TenHuis collection of china cups with no handles, a dog dish for a long-ago pet, an electric percolator with a frayed cord, and other junk. We'd actually dusted the shelves. To prove it, we'd left the dust rag.

Dust rag was the right name for the old towel I saw on the bottom shelf. The fabric was permeated with dust and stained with grease. Gross. I shoved the rag aside.

And under it was a roll of duct tape.

I picked it up. They say duct tape can do anything, but I didn't see how it could get that window frame out without making any noise.

Joe was speaking softly. "It would be a snap to get this window out, if we just didn't have to be quiet."

"How?"

"Break the glass."

"What about the frames that hold the panes in place?"

"Those are flimsy. I could yank those out in a heartbeat—if it weren't for the glass. But if I take this iron bar to the glass, the television isn't going to hide the noise when it breaks. Besides, we'd have glass all over the place."

I looked again at the duct tape. I found the end and scratched at it with my fingernail. What if the tape had been there twenty years and was completely dried up?

I got hold of the end and pulled the tape back. It came loose with a satisfying rasp. I nearly forgot to whisper. "Joe!"

Joe whirled toward me. He stared at the duct tape. He breathed hard; then he hobbled the two steps it took to reach me, and he threw his arms around me. We stood there hugging each other.

His lips were near my ear. "Where did you find that?"

"On the bottom shelf. Under a rag."

"I lost that roll of duct tape when we were working down

here last summer. I looked everywhere and finally went out to the truck and got a new roll. And all the time it was lurking here, waiting to save our lives."

He hopped back to the window and in three minutes he had each pane of the window plastered with two layers of duct tape.

"Now," he said. "We have to pray that breaking the window doesn't make so much noise that Patricia Youngman comes down here."

"How about if I make a commotion? Bang on the door."

"Too dangerous. If she fires through the door . . ."

"If we can unscrew the rest of that bed frame, I can throw bed knobs at the door."

I dragged the bed frame over, both head and foot, and Joe and I unscrewed the sixteen iron knobs somebody had thought were ornamental.

Then I positioned myself at the bottom of the stairs. Joe took his place beside the duct-taped window. We counted three. I began to throw the bed knobs at the door at the top of the stairs, two or three at a time, and Joe began to hit the window with the metal rod. Between us, we made a horrible din.

"Help!" I yelled as loudly as I could. "Help! Call an ambulance! Please! He's dying!"

I heard Patricia Youngman's footsteps overhead. She was running through the dining room, into the kitchen. When she reached the back hall—thank God our old house amplifies every sound made in it—I ran around behind the chimney.

When I peeked at Joe, I saw that he had stopped hitting the windows.

Bam! Bam! Two shots plowed through the door. I didn't want to know where they hit.

"Shut up!" Patricia Youngman screamed the words. "I'll be leaving soon. If you stay quiet, I'll slide the bolt open before I go. If you keep yelling, I'll leave you to starve."

She didn't seem to expect an answer. She tromped back through the kitchen, through the dining room, and into the living room. She didn't turn the television off. I'll swear I heard the couch creak when she sat back down.

Joe was pulling the glass out of the window. As he'd hoped, the duct tape had held it together. Only one or two pieces fell to the floor. I picked them up.

He knocked the glass out around the edges, then used the metal bar to break out the small strips of wood that had held the panes in place.

"Now all we have to do is dig out through three feet of snow," he said.

"I can do that. You sit down."

"I'll make you a shovel."

Joe used his pocket knife to dig two or three nails out of one of the flimsy storage shelves. When I again urged him to sit down, he didn't argue. He went back to the stairs and sat down on one of the lower steps.

We were a long way from out of there. At least three feet of snow was piled up on the west side of the house.

I used the board to drag snow into the basement. Luckily, I had gloves in my coat pocket. But I couldn't reach very far outside the window—I may be nearly six feet tall, but that window was even higher than my head. And there was nothing to stand on.

Or was there?

I eyed the wonderful bed frame again. I dragged the headboard—does an iron bedstead have a headboard? Whatever it was called, it would have been at the head of the bed. I pulled it over and propped it against the wall, sideways. Like a ladder.

I looked around to see Joe silently applauding.

By standing on the headboard as if it were a ladder, I was able to reach farther outside the window and drag more snow inside. In a few minutes Joe came over and insisted on taking a turn. In about fifteen minutes the board pushed through to the outside.

Silently, we did a high five.

I got back up on our improvised ladder and enlarged the hole in the snow. By then it was dark outside. I didn't know if that was good or not. If Patricia Youngman looked out a west window, she might be less likely to see us. But there was snow everywhere. Moving figures would be hard to miss against all that white in daytime or at night.

Joe checked the opening. Then he stepped down. "Out you go. But look around carefully before you get out. Then run straight to the trees. Don't get curious and look in a window to see what Patricia's doing."

"No way! All I want is to get away from here. But you go first. It'll be harder for you to get away because of your knee."

"No. I don't want to be a male chauvinist, but my upper body strength is better than yours. I can pull myself out. You'll get out faster if I give you a boost."

"But—"

He put his arms around me. "I promise, Lee. I'll be right out. Come on. We'll have to use your jacket to pad the frame. There's still some glass."

I climbed up, took off my jacket, and laid it across the bottom of the window frame. I climbed up the bedstead ladder and put my head and shoulder through. Joe boosted me up, then gave a terrific push on my bottom. Before I could realize what was happening, I was rolling in the snow underneath our bedroom windows. As instructed, I got to my feet and ran across the lawn to the trees. Once among them, I huddled behind a large evergreen and looked back.

Sure enough, Joe's head emerged—more slowly than mine had. He pulled himself out on the lawn. He twisted around and stuck his head back down the tunnel that led to the window. For a moment I thought he was going back inside. Then he was on his feet, waving my jacket in one hand. He staggered through the snow.

He'd almost reached the trees when headlights turned into our lane.

Talk about heart palpitations. Mine was racing with the same irregular rhythm of Joe's limping run.

Patricia Youngman had obviously been waiting for something or someone. This car had to be her appointment.

I didn't even care who it was. I was only afraid that Joe would get caught in the headlights.

Joe obviously saw the danger. If you can stagger and run, he did it. By the time the lights reached the lawn, he was nearly to the trees. He fell down on my jacket and lay still. He told me later he was trying to visualize himself as a log.

Apparently his effort worked, because the vehicle drove slowly by. Of course, it had so far been only a set of headlights to me, but as it drew up opposite our front door, the porch light abruptly came on.

Now I could see the vehicle. It was a white Cadillac Escalade.

Rhett?

The Escalade stopped, and a window went down. Sure enough, after Patricia Youngman said something indistinguishable, Rhett's voice came wafting over the snow. "Around to the side? Okay."

He drove on. I plunged out from behind my bush and helped Joe to his feet. I tugged at him, trying to get him into the trees.

"Not so fast," he whispered. "I nearly did my knee in with that belly flop."

He got into the trees somehow. I found a log and dusted the snow off of it. Then I draped my jacket around his shoulders and tried to get him to sit on the log.

But Joe was fumbling in his pocket. "Here." He thrust his cell phone into my hand.

"You had a cell phone all the time?" My whisper was angry.

"Yes. I tried using it as soon as I fell down the steps. No service."

"Oh."

"It didn't seem tactful to bring it up when we couldn't use it."

Shielding the phone from the house—I didn't want Patricia to look out and see suspicious lights in the woods—I checked. Still no service. I silently cursed our cell phone carrier. Our phones worked reliably only from the second floor. Why, oh, why hadn't Patricia Youngman locked us upstairs?

I whispered again. "Can you walk over to the Baileys' house?"

"Not the Baileys'. That's the wrong direction. We'd have to pass the living room windows. You'd probably better go without me. Go to the Garretts' house. If they're not home and the cell phone won't work there, Dick told me there's a key wired to that little holly bush by the step."

"But—"

"When you get to a phone, call the cops. Then call this number." He repeated it twice.

I parroted it back. "Who's that?"

"It's the FBI."

"Joe, how did you just happen to know the FBI's phone number?"

"I'll tell you later. The faster you can get the cops here, the sooner we'll be safe. I'll follow you, but I can't hurry. You've got to do it."

I did it. I left the shelter of the trees, and I ran alongside them until I got to the drive. Then I ran down the drive—or I tiptoed beside the drive. It had been plowed, but there were still icy patches. A bad fall could be deadly.

I got to Lake Shore Drive, crossed it, and did my tiptoe act down the Garretts' drive. It was longer than ours. And darker. And just as slippery. There are streetlights here and there in our part of Warner Pier, but the darn trees keep the light from reaching the ground, even in the winter, when most of the trees are bare.

Periodically, I checked Joe's phone. There was still no service.

The Garretts have a security light in their drive, and the snow around their Craftsman-style bungalow sparkled like diamonds in its glare. Their walk had been cleared, and their porch swept. There was a light in the living room.

But no one answered the door.

I pounded on it three times, but no one came to greet me. No one moved across the living room.

The holly bush. I turned to it, but before I tackled searching it for a wired-on key, I tried Joe's phone one more time. There was one bar of service.

If only I were a little higher up.

I jumped off the porch and went racing around the house, plunging through the snow. When Garnet and Dick Garrett took over her family's summer cottage, they remodeled it. One addition was a second-story deck on the back of the house, a deck that was higher than the trees blocking their view of Lake Michigan. Joe and I had attended the party they held to inaugurate that deck.

There was snow on the steps, but I was able to brush it off and climb up. I checked the phone one more time. Oh, glory! Three bars.

I called the Warner Pier police dispatcher. After five o'clock, 9-1-1 calls were handled by the county sheriff's office, thirty miles away. But I stayed on the line until I was sure the dispatcher grasped the situation, and until I was sure she understood that I was asking that no sirens be used.

"We want to catch these people," I said. "Not let them get away."

"Right. Now, stay on the line."

"No. I have to make another call."

The FBI. Joe had told me to call the FBI. I didn't understand why. But he had even known the number.

I called it.

The voice that answered was curt. "Yes."

"This is Lee Woodyard," I said. "Joe Woodyard's wife. He told me to call."

"Yes?"

"Patricia Youngman is in our house. Joe and I managed to

get out. Joe is hurt. Youngman is meeting with Rhett Spivey. He just drove up."

"What are—"

"I can't talk anymore. The cops are on the way. You're invited, too. No sirens! I've got to get back to Joe."

I punched the phone off and started back down the snowy steps of the deck. I skidded down the Garretts' road, across Lake Shore Drive, and back down our drive. I kept a close eye for a vehicle coming toward me—whether it was a Cadillac Escalade or my van or Joe's truck, I didn't want to get caught on that drive.

When I got to our lawn, I took off through the snow, following my own tracks back to the spot where I'd left Joe. I wasn't surprised when he wasn't there. After all, he had said he would follow me as quickly as his knee would allow.

Feeling like an Indian tracker, I tried to figure out which way he had gone by looking at footprints in the snow.

I didn't think Joe would have gone through the woods. The terrain was simply too rough for that to be practical. So I looked in the snow between the trees and the house. For one thing, the porch light and what little light there was from the sky gave me a slight amount of visibility there.

And sure enough, I saw Joe's tracks coming out of the trees. I expected them to turn toward the drive, basically taking the same route I had taken.

But they didn't. They went straight across the yard and back to the house.

At first I thought I was imagining that. It seemed ludicrous. But I kept looking. There was my set of tracks, running from the house with toes pointed toward the trees. There were Joe's tracks, following the same route. And there was another set of Joe's tracks, headed back to the house.

Nose to ground like a bloodhound, I moved across the yard. Joe's second set of tracks led right to that window he and I had used to escape. Light was pouring out of it, logically enough, since we hadn't turned out the ceiling bulb when we climbed out.

My jacket was back on the window frame. I flopped down and looked inside.

I could see Joe on the other side of the basement. Joe had gone back inside.

Why had he done that? I could have wrung his neck.

Well, I wasn't going to find out lying on my stomach out in the snow. I turned around and scooted into the window feet-first.

Finding the bedstead we'd used as a ladder wasn't too easy, but I managed to get my feet on it without knocking it over with a clang.

I turned to see Joe at the other end of the cellar, glaring at me and motioning me back outside. I ignored his actions. I tiptoed toward him. He made the universal signal for silence, putting his finger to his lips. Then he pointed above his head. And I heard Patricia Youngman's voice.

I realized Joe had come back inside the cellar so he could eavesdrop on Patricia and Rhett.

Chapter 20

But the voice I heard wasn't Patricia's. It wasn't Rhett's either.

It was a gruff, angry voice. It took me a moment to identify it as the voice that had answered the mysterious number someone had called from TenHuis Chocolade, the long distance number I'd never been able to identify.

I looked at Joe. Maybe he knew who that person was. I'd given the mysterious phone number to Hogan, telling him I suspected that Pamela—now revealed in her true identity as Patricia Youngman—had called it. He'd never told me what he found out.

"And just how many copies of it have you made?" the gruff voice said.

"None. I'm dealing openly here." That was Patricia Youngman.

"Sure you are." The words were sarcastic.

"We'll just have to trust each other."

The gruff voice gave a gruff laugh.

"Why shouldn't we trust each other?" Patricia sounded completely calm. "We did for years."

"Until you stabbed me in the back."

"Until I discovered I had been picked as the one to be

thrown to the feds. When I was the only one who hadn't gotten a slice of the pie."

Patricia's voice had grown angry, but she stopped and when she spoke again she seemed to have regained control of herself. "But now you realize just how much I know. And that I can prove it. Do you want the records or not?"

"I don't have much choice."

"I'm glad you recognize that. As soon as the money is in my account, you'll receive the evidence."

"How will you get it to me?"

"Don't worry. You'll get it."

"The damn FBI has me completely sewed up. My mail, my telephones . . . I had to bribe Rhett to sneak me out of the house tonight!"

"Don't worry! You'll get the evidence."

"But how?"

"What you don't know, you can't mention on a tapped phone. I'll get it to you!"

There was a long silence—well, about thirty seconds. But it seemed long. Then the gruff voice spoke. "Okay."

"Then I think we're through here. You have the account number. As soon as you take action, I'll deliver the records. You can leave the way you came."

The guy with the gruff voice didn't reply. We heard his footsteps cross the living room, the dining room, the kitchen. He slammed the back door angrily.

Patricia Youngman stayed in the living room. She crossed to the front door.

I whispered in Joe's ear, "What's she doing?"

He whispered back, "I don't know, but it's time for us to get out that window again."

"Where are the cops I called?"

"I don't know that either."

We started for the window, and I heard the motor of a car outside. It must have been Rhett leaving. Then Patricia Youngman's steps strode through the living room and across the dining room.

I was sure she was headed for the basement door.

Was she going to simply unlock the bolt, so we could leave? Somehow I didn't think so.

"Turn off the light," Joe said.

I ran for the light switch. The darkness was absolute at first. Then I could see the faint light from the hot water tank's burner.

"Get to the window," Joe whispered.

I held my hands straight out and walked across the basement until I hit the wall. I almost tripped over the bedstead propped up under the window. I expected to run into Joe at the window, but I didn't.

"Where are you?" I whispered.

The darkness was slightly less dense by then, and I saw movement under the basement stairs. It had to be Joe.

"Joe!"

"Get out, Lee!"

Patricia Youngman was at the basement door. I could hear the bolt slide back.

Maybe I should have obeyed Joe and climbed out the window. But I knew Patricia Youngman was going to hit the light switch at the top of the stairs any second. Then, as soon as she took two or three steps down, she'd be able to see the whole basement, and she'd be holding Sarajane's pistol.

I had only a moment to get out the window. It wasn't long enough.

The thought of my fanny framed in the window when Patricia Youngman raised that pistol—well, I couldn't make myself climb out. Besides, I'd be leaving Joe behind. He would have no way to escape from a woman with a firearm.

If Joe and I rushed her together, maybe we'd have a chance.

I moved toward the stairs, toward where I thought Joe was standing.

But I had taken only a couple of steps away from the window escape route when the door opened, and the overhead light flashed on. Patricia Youngman came down the stairs, bending over, looking around.

I was right out in the middle of the room; there was no way she could miss seeing me.

She did see me, and she laughed.

What she didn't see was Joe, standing under the stairs. His head was even with her ankles.

Patricia came down two more steps. Now Joe's head was even with her knees.

Then she saw the open window behind me. "You little devil!" she said. "You almost got out the window!"

She aimed her pistol at me.

I stared, mesmerized. There was no place to hide, nothing to jump behind.

Joe swung the leg of that wonderful bedstead. Aiming through the space between the steps and using what looked like a tennis backhand, he hit a mighty blow at the side of Patricia Youngman's knee.

She fell sideways, pitching down the last four steps and landing on the little cement pad at the bottom of the basement steps.

She screamed. Her pistol went off. I don't know where the bullet went, but it didn't hit me, and it didn't hit Joe.

I ran toward her, and so did Joe. I stood on her arm, and Joe grabbed the gun away.

Patricia lay in the sand, sobbing. "My knee!" she screamed. "My shoulder! My arm! You've broken my knee!"

"Fair enough," Joe answered. "You tried to break mine."

I heard the kitchen door fly open. Feet pounded on the floor above our heads. Yells rang out. "FBI!" "Police!"

"Finally," I said. I went up the steps.

"Better keep your hands up," Joe said. "The FBI might not know you're one of the good guys."

I guess they figured it out when Hogan ran over and scooped me into a giant hug. "Lee! Lee!"

"Quick!" I said. "Go downstairs! Joe's standing on top of Patricia Youngman!"

Things got a bit confused then. At least ten law enforcement types rushed into the house, plus a half-dozen EMTs a few minutes later, after two ambulances arrived. Hogan told me that other lawmen were taking care of Marson Endicott— yes, he was the guy with the gruff voice.

Endicott had been arrested as he left our drive, Hogan said. "They also picked up that butler guy, Rhett Spivey," he said. "He apparently hid Endicott in the back of his SUV so he could get out of the Dome Home."

"Why didn't Patricia Youngman just have Rhett sneak her into the Dome Home?" I said.

Hogan looked surprised. "Spivey might have blabbed."

"I don't think so. After all, they went to college together. They exchanged class rings. I think he was her spy inside the Dome Home all along."

Hogan blinked. "How'd you figure that out?"

"Internet. When Myrl Sawyer rousted Patricia out of bed to leave here in a hurry, Patricia lost the ring. I found it when I stripped her bed. In fact, it's in the vase on the mantel. I came back to get it; that was why she caught me. Anyway, Rhett had a similar ring he wore on his pinkie. I used the Internet to figure out what college the rings came from, and I found out Rhett and Patricia graduated the same year. I left you a message about it."

Hogan had the grace to look a bit shamedfaced. "Sorry. I've been too busy to check my messages."

By the time they carried Patricia Youngman out, handcuffed to a gurney, she had stopped yelling and sobbing. One of the EMTs knew Hogan and stopped to speak. "I don't think she's hurt bad," he said. "Just bruised up. But we'll get a doctor to look at her."

"Keep your eye on her."

"We'll have these guys with the FBI jackets along."

Joe got a better diagnosis from the EMTs, after they saw that he could move his knee easily, despite the swelling. It looked like a bad sprain, they said. The bleeding came from a badly skinned knee. They still wanted to load him into a second ambulance and take him in for an X-ray.

"No." Joe's voice was firm. "I'll go to the doctor tomorrow."

That didn't make me happy. "Joe! This injury could be serious."

"I'm not going to the emergency room. Have you forgotten? We're due at Mom's house for dinner. Right now."

"She'll understand."

"I know. But I want to get this little family meeting over with. I'll see the doctor tomorrow. Just give me a king-sized

Band-Aid and an ice pack and help me get into some clean pants."

While Hogan was ordering the law enforcement vehicles out of our drive, the FBI agent who seemed to be in charge followed Joe into the bedroom to quiz him about what he'd heard while he was listening from the basement.

"That was a stupid thing to do, Woodyard," he said. "Once you were out of the house, you should have stayed out."

"I know," Joe said. "But it was obvious that Patricia Youngman had set up some sort of meeting in our house. Normally, neither Lee nor I would be home that time of day, so it was a good enough spot for it. It was simply bad luck that we both came home. That forced her to lock us in the basement.

"Once we got out, I was extremely curious about what she was up to. This house is like—the inside of a drum, I guess. There are no secrets. Anything that's said anyplace inside can be heard anyplace else inside. I couldn't resist eavesdropping. And it was my house. I didn't need a warrant."

"As long as you were listening, what did you hear?"

"She and Endicott were making final arrangements for a payoff. He was to pay a substantial sum into an offshore account. Then she would send him 'the records.' "

"She didn't say where those records are now?"

"Oh, no! She was too cagey for that."

I thought about it. "Records" could take a million forms—anything from a ledger or diary to a computer disk.

If I were Patricia Youngman, I asked myself, where would I hide "records," records that could bring a major corporation down and send its top executives to jail?

I didn't think I'd put them in a safety-deposit box. I might want them on a Sunday, for example, and bank robberies get so complicated. No, I'd want to keep them with me. Wear them in a locket maybe.

Well, they would search Patricia Youngman to the skin when they got her to the hospital or to the jail. In the meantime, I needed to get the box of chocolates I was taking to Mercy's house . . .

"Oh, my gosh!" I said. "She put the records on the end table!"

The FBI agent stared at me. I led him into the living room and pointed to the end table. On it was a small tube of M&M Minis.

"Don't touch it!" I said. "You'll want to check it for fingerprints."

The FBI guy—I didn't learn his name until later—frowned. "Why?"

"Because through all her identities—Pamela, Christina, and Patricia—Ms. Youngman always carried a tube of M&M Minis. She was working at TenHuis Chocolade, where we were making fabulous chocolates, and each employee could have two samples every day. But she always bypassed our scrumptious truffles and bonbons for those M&M Minis you can buy at the grocery store. That tube is exactly the right size to hold the flash drive for a computer, and it's something she could have in her purse or pocket without raising questions."

The FBI man called for an evidence bag.

While I had his attention, I asked another question. "But who hired PDQ Investigations?"

Hogan had reappeared, and he chuckled. "Patricia Youngman hired them to find herself," he said.

"That's crazy!"

"After Myrl Sawyer was killed, we were able to get some of those 'underground railroad' women to open up. It seems that Patricia Youngman had donated money to their cause for years, so she knew how to get in touch with them. But, of course, they wouldn't help someone like her hide out. They only help abused wives they are convinced are actually in danger. So Patricia decided to find such a person and exchange places with them. She hired PDQ Investigations to find Christina Meachum."

"She must have looked for her specifically, because they did have a superficial resemblance to each other," I said. "I should have figured out that Pamela was using that odd eye makeup as a masquerade. I guess she wore brown contact lenses and stuffed cotton or something in her cheek, too. I know that the night she stayed here, she was careful not to let me see her without makeup."

"That could be. We speculate that Youngman got Christina Meachum to take her place and flee to Namibia. Then she inserted herself into the underground railroad as a 'victim.' The problem, of course, was that she couldn't let anyone who knew her as Patricia see her."

I nodded. "I remember that when she came face-to-face with Myrl, Myrl gasped. Then she laughed. I guess Patricia knew then that she'd have to kill Myrl. She must have already prepared a hideout by stealing Dolly's keys from my desk. And, of course, she was lying when she told Sarajane Harding that someone had called her at the Peach Street B&B. She just wanted an excuse to get out of the underground railroad."

"I'm sure that's right."

"But how did Patricia Youngman get the underground railroad to send her to Warner Pier?"

"I haven't got the answer to that one. Apparently Sarajane's house is a regular stop on the railroad, and Youngman must have jimmied the deal somehow—forced them to send her there. But it was a convenient spot for meeting Endicott, since he had a house here."

"But why did she blow it with phone calls? I'm sure that's how PDQ Investigations found her."

"Huh." Hogan made a contemptuous sound. "Youngman forgot that she was dealing with a bunch of sleazeballs. She hired PDQ to find Christina Meachum—who was not involved with the underground railway or the Federal Witness Protection Program. She was just hiding out on her own. Then PDQ sold the information to Harold Belcher. Of course, by then, Christina had moved on. So Belcher paid them to continue the search."

By then Joe was limping out wearing clean clothes and carrying a cold pack provided by the EMTs. I was also relieved when one of Hogan's patrolmen reported that Dolly's Jeep had been found in our neighbors' drive.

We left the law in charge of our house and headed for Joe's mom's house in my van.

After we turned onto Lake Shore Drive, I began to quiz Joe. "How did you get involved with the FBI?"

"You know how Hogan feels about them, of course."

"He says all local lawmen regard them with suspicion."

"Hogan certainly does. But they've been investigating Marson Endicott for a long time, and when Endicott came to the Dome Home, they set up wiretaps and so forth. In cases like that, protocol requires that they touch base with local law enforcement."

"But that would be Hogan's problem. How would it involve you?"

Joe chuckled. "As the husband of Hogan's step-niece."

"Huh?"

"Hogan wanted a witness to his dealings with them, but he was afraid that if he got one of his patrolmen involved, word would leak out. He could swear me to secrecy."

"Were the FBI agents staying at the Lake Michigan Inn?"

"Yep. They had a listening station set up out there."

"For the wiretaps?"

"Not only wiretaps. A wire."

"A wire? You mean they had an informant?"

"Right. Elliot J. Smith, the CFO who probably came up with the whole scheme to loot the Prodigal Corporation."

"Potty Mouth!"

"That's him. Now he's scrambling to cut a deal and avoid prison. You can see why Hogan and I were so firm about not mentioning him being in Hogan's office."

We both laughed. "Now," I said, "let's put this whole thing out of our minds until your mom and Mike have had time to announce whatever they've called us together to announce."

"Yeah. Our day might have been a little more exciting than theirs. Besides, I have an announcement of my own."

"What's that?"

He told me.

Of course, our plan to say nothing to Mercy, Mike, Lindy, and Tony about the afternoon's excitement didn't work. As mayor, Mike had his ear out, and he'd already heard about the big FBI raid on our house. Joe's sprained knee was also hard to ignore. But after a flurry of conversation and concern, we were able to eat dinner. Then Mike and Mercy broke out the champagne and made their announcement.

A cruise. We were to go to the Caribbean during spring break for Warner Pier schools—all six adults plus Lindy and Tony's three kids. The wedding was to be on the ship.

"Just quiet," Mercy said. "We're not inviting all the passengers and crew."

March. The end of the Michigan winter. A perfect time and the perfect reason to get out of town.

After we'd all stopped hooting, whooping, hugging, and kissing, they got down to the financial plans they'd made. It was fairly complicated, but it boiled down to requiring that all businesses be sold in case of the death of one or the other spouse. Money from the sales would go to the particular partner's son.

I could see the relief in Tony's face when he saw that his dad didn't expect him to take over his restaurant business. And maybe a little relief in Joe's face when he learned he wouldn't be responsible for an insurance agency—except for selling it.

"Of course," Mike said, "we're planning on living so long and so well that none of you gets a penny. And as for my personal plans—well . . ."

"Wait a minute," Joe said. "I have an announcement myself."

"Oh?"

"I'm resigning as city attorney."

Mike looked dismayed.

"The job's been a godsend, Mike. You helped me get it, and I'll always be grateful. But it's time to move on. Beginning

April 1, I'm joining the staff of West Michigan Defense—a new nonprofit legal agency. My buddy Webb Bartlett is one of the founders. I'll work two days a week." Joe grinned. "Or that's the theory."

I felt tears well up. Joe could have joined Webb's firm—or even Marty Ludlum's firm—and made a lot more money. But Joe is still true to his college dream of helping people who really need help to navigate the legal system.

I love that guy. And luckily, I love the chocolate business, because I'm not quitting anytime soon.

Chocolate Chat
Making Handmade Chocolates

Chocolatiers begin making handmade bonbons by molding their thin outer shells. To do this, melted chocolate is poured into a mold that looks something like an ice tray. As soon as each cavity is filled to the top, the tray is turned over and the chocolate poured back out into the bowl it came from. This leaves thin shells called "bakjes." (Pronounced "bah-kees.") After the bakjes are firmly set, the filling is poured into them. Again, the future bonbons set until they are firm. Then each is covered with chocolate.

Handmade truffles begin with fondant filling rolled into a ball between the palms. In a professional shop, it's important that each ball be uniform. These are covered with chocolate.

Two methods are used to cover truffles or bonbons with chocolate: They may either be hand-dipped or "enrobed," which means run through a sort of shower bath of melted chocolate called "couverture." The final step for both types of chocolates is decoration—either with chocolate in special designs or with nuts or other embellishments.